# Montana Cowboy Christmas

# MONTANA COWBOY CHRISTMAS

## A Wyatt Brothers Romance

### JANE PORTER

TULE
PUBLISHING

## Dedication

For Cyndi, so very glad to have you in my corner always!
Love you!

Dear Readers,

I grew up in a family with strong Christmas traditions. My dad, a professor, loved Christmas so much that every year he earmarked his December paycheck as his—my mom got the other eleven months to pay bills—but his December paycheck was for Christmas: the tree, presents, decorations.

I was fifteen when he died, and my brothers and sister became even more important to me. They were truly 'my family' and so as we got older and began to go to college, and then later fall in love and get married, it was hard for me to accept that we wouldn't all be together for the holidays. It simply didn't feel right not to have everyone there on Christmas Eve or Christmas morning. Being a newlywed and discovering your new family didn't celebrate Christmas your way, was also a shock. I missed my family's traditions and how special Christmas had felt. Happily as a mom, I've been able to recreate so many of those traditions and memories from my childhood, and I hope you're passing down your favorite traditions, too!

I also hope you will enjoy my newest Christmas story, a story of family, love, and second chances…my favorite kind!

Happy Holidays!
Jane

*"And we know that all things work together for good to those who love Him."*

Romans 8:28.

# CHAPTER ONE

SAM WYATT DIDN'T feel like leaving bed, not when it was warm and his room was cold, but without getting out of bed there would be no coffee, and he liked his morning coffee almost as much as he liked his boots and horse.

Going downstairs meant he'd see family, and he wasn't sure he was ready for that either, not after last night's rowdy family dinner. The Wyatts' had a lot of strong personalities and, put the four Wyatt brothers together—along with Mom and Granddad—things got loud, and heated, fast.

Billy and Tommy had always enjoyed stirring things up, while Sam liked things calm. Consistent. He was more like Joe in that respect, and more of a loner like Joe. Except Joe had gotten married earlier in the year, and surprise, surprise, had fallen in love with his mail-order bride and was far happier now than Sam had ever known him to be.

Sam *was* happy for Joe. Maybe a little envious, too, but Sam didn't feel much like exploring that thought—now or ever. He'd learned serious relationships were work, requiring constant compromise and sacrifice, and he wasn't sure he was built for compromise, or sacrifice, anymore.

No, he liked his solitude, and he was looking forward to having his own place. He was scheduled to close on his new Wyoming ranch the day after Christmas. Sam pictured his property outside Cody. Hills, pastures, land. Lots of land. Good barns, stable, solid house. Nothing luxurious but it had everything he needed for a successful business. Sam knew cattle, and he couldn't wait until he could build his own herds.

Leaving bed, he stepped into flannel pajama pants and tugged a sweatshirt over his head, wincing at the pain streaking through his shoulder. He'd reinjured his shoulder last week during the NFRs in Las Vegas: but he couldn't complain, having walked away from this year's National Finals Rodeo as world champion in tie-down roping and third in steer wrestling. Younger brothers Billy and Tommy had been there, too, and all three Wyatts' had left with serious money, but this was Sam's year, and earning a quarter of a million dollars went a long way to compensating for a torn rotator cuff.

Downstairs, the kitchen was pleasantly warm and empty. Sam reached into the cupboard for painkillers, washing the tablets down with a half glass of water, before filling his coffee cup.

Maybe he should just do the surgery, get it over with. Letting his shoulder heal on its own could take ten to twelve weeks. But he had four weeks, not twelve, before the new season began. Problem was, surgery wasn't always successful.

In his head, Sam planned his day. His mom's birthday was a week from today, and Christmas was ten days away. Sam planned on going into Marietta and getting some shopping done, and then he'd stop in at the bank and make sure money was ready to be wired from his account so they could close on the Cody ranch on time.

Tommy and Billy knew about the property in Cody, but Sam still needed to tell the rest of the family. He trusted there wouldn't be hard feelings. Joe might say he was upset, but Joe was married now and would soon have kids and the ranch would belong to his kids. That was just how it worked.

Floorboards squeaked overhead and he glanced up to the ceiling, the room directly above the kitchen belonging to his younger brothers. A minute later, Tommy descended the stairs, entering the kitchen in baggy sweatpants and nothing else. It was a little cool to be without a shirt but Tommy loved showing off his body, especially his eight-pack abs. Sam arched an eyebrow, silently mocking Tommy's choice of attire.

Tommy grinned. "Don't be jealous. You can't all be me."

"Not jealous, Tom. I'm all right being who I am."

"Guess who I saw last night?" Tommy asked, reaching for one of the glossy red and white Santa mugs lining the wide lip of the kitchen window, mugs that Joe's new wife, Sophie, had put there, along with the plethora of Christmas decorations all over the house. They'd never done much decorating at Christmas, but it seemed no one had the heart to tell Sophie that.

Sam didn't take the bait and just waited as Tommy filled his glossy red Santa mug and then replaced the coffee carafe.

"Why didn't you take one of the Christmas mugs?" Tommy asked.

"There was no Grinch mug," Sam answered easily, lifting his brown feed mug with the faded logo. "Had to make do with this."

"Sophie is excited about the new mugs."

"I noticed."

"You don't like Christmas anymore?"

"I like it just fine. Now, who did you see last night?"

"You'll never figure it out; not in a million years."

"Put like that, just tell me."

Tommy lifted his cup. "Make at least one guess. Humor me."

"I humor you all the time."

"Dang, you're a grouch." Tommy paused, took a sip, and then another, all the while eyeing Sam over the rim of the smiling Santa. "I was at the Wolf Den, does that help?"

Sam suppressed a sigh. The Wolf Den was the seediest bar in town, probably the seediest bar anywhere in a forty-mile radius. Truckers, bikers, and troublemakers liked to frequent the place. He personally avoided it, but his brother had been there for a birthday party last night. His youngest brother liked to run a little wild still. "I don't know since it's not a place I like to go."

"I'll help you out. Someone you dated."

This caught Sam's attention. Someone he dated was working at the Wolf Den? He hadn't dated that many people, not growing up. Back in high school, there had been just two girls. Sam tended to settle into serious relationships, long relationships, rather than playing the field like Tommy. So if it was someone he dated, that meant it had to be Heather or Caitlin. But, Heather was married with four little ones, and Caitlin had moved away, somewhere in Texas, working for a big tech company. She'd always been smart, ambitious, and she'd gone off to college and never returned. But had she finally come back?

"Caitlin?" Sam asked. "Is she working at the Wolf Den?"

"Nope."

"I don't know anyone else from Marietta I've dated."

"I didn't say she was from Marietta."

Sam frowned. "I don't know. I give up."

"It's Ivy. Ivy was bartending last night."

Sam's jaw clenched and his stomach felt hard, tight as he slowly set his mug down. "Say that again."

"Saw Ivy last night." Tommy wasn't smiling anymore. "And it was her, I know it was her. I even asked one of the waitresses. It's your Ivy."

"Did you talk to her?"

"No."

"Did she see you?" Sam asked.

"I don't know. Once, I thought I saw her looking at me, but when I looked her in the eye, she glanced away and…" His voice faded. He shrugged. "To be honest, it just felt really weird and awkward. I think she was surprised see me, and I don't think she was happy to see me, and suddenly I didn't want to be there." Tommy went to the fridge, pulled out the carton of half-and-half, and poured a generous measure into his cup. "She looked different, too. Hard to explain. She just didn't look like your girlfriend anymore."

Sam grabbed the half-and-half carton and returned it to the fridge, closing the refrigerator door with a little more force than necessary. "That's because she isn't *my* girlfriend. She hasn't been *my* Ivy for two years now."

"Are you going to go see her? She's working again tonight."

Sam gave his brother an incredulous look. "No, I'm not going to see her. Why would I do that?"

"Because once you two were serious, really serious. We all thought you were going to marry her." Tommy paused, waited. "*You* even thought you were going to marry her."

"Doesn't matter. It didn't happen. She moved on, and I moved on, and we're both in a better place."

Tommy took his cup and walked across the room, grabbing a chair from the kitchen table and pulling it out. "But are you?" he demanded, sitting down. "Are you really in a better place? Cause you could have fooled me."

"Mind your own business, Tom."

"I normally do."

"So butt out."

Tommy said nothing for a long moment, concentrating on his coffee, making a show of taking slow appreciative sips. His broad, bare shoulders twisted, shifting the thick scar wrapped around his rib cage. "You know best. Maybe she's not your girl now, but you still have a soft spot for her, and if it doesn't bother you that she's working in a modern-day whorehouse—"

"Wolf Den is a strip bar, not a whore house. And I thought you said Ivy was a bartender, not a pole dancer."

Tom shrugged. "You know the kind of guys that go there—"

"Guys like you."

Tommy just smiled, a dimple forming deep in his lean cheek. He gave his brother a look of pure pleasure. There was love in his expression, but also a challenge. They'd grown up loving each other, fighting each other, besting each other. It was just the Wyatt way. "Yeah guys like me, but because *I* know who Ivy is, I wasn't hitting on her, and I wasn't saying anything, and I wasn't propositioning her. No sir, I kept my distance, and I was respectful, but Ivy is beautiful. Guys hit on her. They think she's hot. I've got to tell you, she was getting a lot of attention last night, more attention than the dancers, more attention than the cocktail waitresses in their skimpy outfits and Ivy was just Ivy, in jeans and a T-shirt—" He broke off, shrugged. "Sure it was tight, not that I was looking, but others were. She's got that body—"

"Enough about her body," Sam growled.

"Sure, Sam, whatever you say. But before I shut up alto-gether, let me just add, that if you really care about Ivy—and you might not, because you're right, you loved her a couple years ago and maybe you didn't really love her, maybe it was just infatuation, maybe it was just a passing phase—but if you were ever her *friend*, I would check in on her, and make sure she's okay." And with that Tommy stood, grabbed his cup, and walked out of the room, leaving Sam alone.

IVY PULLED ON her heaviest coat, slipped her hands into mittens, and stepped outside to walk to work. It was a beautiful Montana morning, with a crystal-clear blue sky and just a few white clouds scattered above. She was opening the bar this morning and she sang to herself as she walked, *"Over the river and through the woods to the Wolf Den bar I go…"*

Ivy's teeth chattered as a gust of frigid wind tried to knock her off her feet. Just a few more days and she'd have enough to pay for the new transmission her truck needed, and then she'd be able to drive again to work, and to see Scotch, and everything would be much, much easier.

But until then, she'd keep walking to work, which hon-estly, wasn't that bad, as it was only ten minutes from her lodging on Chance Avenue to the Wolf Den bar. Sure, the road was dirty with black snow and salt and ice, but the fresh air always cleared her head and filled her lungs and made her grateful to be alive despite the difficult past few years, because honestly, things could be so much worse. She had a place to live, she was healthy and strong, and earning decent money. Once her truck had a new tranny, she'd have a lot more freedom, and would be in a better position for making decisions about the future. When she'd first arrived in Crawford County, it was supposed to just be for the fall and winter, but now, it was beginning to feel like home and maybe it could be. Maybe this was where she was meant to put down roots.

Ivy just had to stay patient and keep her faith. All good things came to those who believed.

And she believed.

She also believed that Jeb Kruse was taking good care of Scotch. He'd promised to, and why wouldn't he? Just because Jeb had to lay her off didn't mean he was a bad person.

Reaching the Wolf Den, Ivy stamped the dirty snow off her boots before opening the front door. The interior was dim and quiet, but it still had the pungent odor of beer and whiskey.

Pia, one of the cocktail waitresses, was already inside, leaning on the bar reading the paper. She glanced up as Ivy hung her coat on the rack. "Did you hear about Ashley Howe? That little girl from Belgrade who got hurt back in

September?"

"What's happened?" Ivy asked, stashing her purse under the counter because Ivy knew far more about Ashley and the Howe family than she'd ever let on. Last September, Ivy had sold her mare Belle to help Ashley get the therapy the girl needed after her injury. Ivy's donation to Ashley's Go Fund Me had been anonymous. Only the family and Ivy knew what she'd done, and she intended to keep it that way.

"Well, she's coming home from Florida where she's been doing rehab." Pia folded the *Copper Mountain Courier* and slid it across the counter toward Ivy. "She's going to be home for Christmas. That's pretty awesome, don't you think?"

"I do." Ivy washed her hands and dried them and reached for the paper. "Her family will be so happy to have her home with them."

"Do you think she can walk now?"

Ivy hesitated. "I don't know that walking was ever in the cards for her."

"Then why did she go to rehab? I thought they were going to help her walk again?"

"From what I know, rehabilitation after a spinal cord injury involves a lot more than just getting someone to walk. For Ashley, it was probably about making her physically stronger, and helping teach her practical things, like how to get dressed, and how to transfer from a wheelchair on and off a toilet and a bed."

"That's it?"

"That's huge, Pia. She's paralyzed, and these things will help her live more independently."

"That sucks, though. I thought she would maybe be able to walk again. She's just fourteen. Just a kid."

Ivy didn't answer. Ashley's tragic accident had kept her up so many nights. It was so unfair, so unjust. Yes, barrel racing could be a dangerous sport, and injuries occurred, but the fact Ashley was injured in a farming accident, rather than through a riding accident, was just salt in the wound.

Ashley had been a stranger to Ivy before the accident last August. Ivy had never worked with the girl, or her horse, but it didn't matter. She was a talented youth competitor with a passion for the sport, and Ashley's fate was heartbreaking.

Ivy located the article on the front page of the local section and skimmed it. She knew almost everything already. Ashley had finished her ninety days at the center in Florida and was coming home for Christmas. The Howe family was thrilled and had made changes to their house for her, anticipating her arrival. It would be the best Christmas gift for the family to be together again, and according to the article, Ashley's little brothers couldn't wait to have their big sister home as it wouldn't have been Christmas without her.

The aching lump returned to Ivy's throat, and she carefully folded the paper and put it away. She understood missing, understood how Christmas wasn't Christmas without family. This would be Ivy's second Christmas without her mom, and she dreaded the holiday, dreaded it so much that she'd volunteered to work at the Wolf Den to make sure she wasn't alone in her little rented room at Joan's.

Ivy swiped the bar counter with her damp rag, polishing an already-clean surface. She honestly didn't mind bartending at the Wolf Den. She earned big tips, and overtime, and if she kept being frugal, after she got her truck back, she could advertise that she was available for training. It was what she'd grown up doing with her mom, one of the best horse trainers in Montana, if not all of the US. And then eventually, Ivy would buy her own place and board and train horses there.

Either way, much like young Ashley, Ivy's goal was independence. She'd tried relationships and had failed at the last two, and she wasn't going that route again. Better to stand on her own two feet, better to be in control of her life, than let a man try to take over.

She was just checking the kegs and the lines, when the bar's front door opened, pale sunlight spilling across the dark bar floor. She glanced up and saw the silhouette of a cowboy—hat, broad shoulders, tall, lean frame—before she wiped off the spigots, her focus returning to her work. Montana was filled with men and cowboys, but she wasn't interested in any of them. Wes the wolf had cured her of that. He was a mistake she never wanted to repeat.

Boots thudded on the scuffed wooden floor. The cowboy was heading her way. The bar wasn't officially opened for another half hour yet, but she didn't mind an early customer. Management didn't, either. A customer was money and everyone needed money.

She glanced up as he reached the bar. "What can I get you?" she asked, trying to inject some warmth into her voice.

It was only when she looked up that she realized who'd arrived.

Ivy's heart fell, plummeting all the way to the pointed tips of her own boots. For a moment, she thought she might throw up, the shock enormous, and then she got control, and hid her surprise. "Sam Wyatt, what are you doing here?"

"I could say the same for you." He stood, feet planted, hands buried in his coat pockets. "What are you doing at the Wolf Den?"

"Working."

"Yeah, I can see that. But why here? I don't get it."

She pushed her long dark braid off her shoulder. "I was hired to work on the Kruse ranch, training horses, but things got lean, and they laid me off for the winter. They said there might be a job come spring, so here I am."

"Come spring you should be on the road, competing."

"Might do something different this year. Still thinking about my options."

He pulled out a barstool and sat down. "How did you even know about the job on the Kruse ranch? They're not a very big place."

"A friend told me," she said. "Sounded promising, but

you know how it goes. Last one hired, first one fired." She kept her voice casual, even as she avoided eye contact.

Sam was wearing his big black leather jacket, the one with all of the NFR patches. His hat was black, too, and in the shadowy light, he still managed to look impossibly handsome, but then, the Wyatt brothers were not short on looks. Or skill. They were some of the best cowboys in America and they knew it.

Ivy's heart did another weird little flutter and she quickly put a hand to her chest, pressing against the odd painful sensation. She didn't want to feel anything, not when feelings got her into so much trouble.

Sam studied her in silence for a long moment and Ivy stood there, holding her ground, refusing to reveal any of the anxiety she felt.

"What did you say you were drinking?" she asked, voice steady.

"I didn't. But I'll take a beer, bottled."

She'd spent two years with him, two years as Sam's girl, and those two years had been the best years of her life. So, of course she knew his favorite beer, his favorite color, his favorite side of the bed.

Ivy pulled an icy bottle of Coors out from the refrigerator, popped the cap and handed it to him. "I guess Tommy told you I was here."

Sam took a swallow, set the beer down. "He was surprised."

"And he asked you to check on me?" she asked, filled with bittersweet emotion because Tommy and Billy Wyatt had come to mean a lot to her while she and Sam were dating. The four of them traveled together, and by the time she and Sam split, they felt like her brothers, not just his.

"This isn't exactly your kind of place," Sam answered. "Wish you would have let Joe know you needed work. He would have found something for you."

"That wasn't necessary. I found work for me."

*"Here."*

She wasn't going to take the bait. She wouldn't be judged, either. "I make really good money here. Customers tips well." She could tell he didn't like her answer but she didn't care.

The last couple of years had been hard, and the last year, well... that had been beyond brutal, and she owed him nothing, just as he owed her nothing. They'd broken up and they'd gone their separate ways and it had been hard, but she'd moved on. So had he.

"Where's Wes?" Sam asked finally, breaking the long, tense silence.

For the first time since he'd arrived, Ivy looked at Sam, really looked at him, her gaze boring into his as if she could somehow see past the hard blue gaze and the even harder jaw into his soul. But Sam was guarded, and there was never anything she could see, no emotion she could discern.

"No idea," she answered, and that was the truth. She'd

blocked Wes on her phone, blocked him on her social media, and had even stopped updating her social media to keep him from knowing where she was, and if it cost her the rest of her sponsors, well, their money had stopped going into her pockets a long time ago.

"Not very chatty, are you?" he asked.

"Nope." The front door opened and two bikers entered. Ivy nodded at them and then glanced at Sam. "Need anything else?" she asked him.

He shook his head and reached into his back pocket for his wallet.

"Don't bother," she said. "That was on me. Nice to see you, Sam." And then she moved on, walking down the bar to the far end where the bikers had settled and tried to pretend she didn't feel Sam's eyes boring into her back, sending rivulets of sensation up and down her spine, reminding her just how much she'd once wanted him.

Needed him.

"Welcome," she said to the newcomers, flashing a flirty smile. "What can I get you boys?"

SAM HAD INTENDED to Christmas shop after swinging by the Wolf Den, and he tried, too. He drove to Main Street and parked his truck, stalking into the Western Wear store to see if he couldn't find a new Pendleton shirt for Grandad, and maybe a warm soft vest for Mom, but as he surveyed the racks of clothes, he saw Ivy in her tight T-shirt smiling at the bikers, giving them the smile she'd always saved for him.

That sweet, sexy smile made him see red.

He was not happy.

Seriously. Not. Happy.

"Can I help you find something?" the older saleslady asked, approaching Sam.

Sam's narrowed gaze swept from the offending racks of clothes to the saleswoman. He forced himself to soften his expression. "No. Thank you."

"We have some good Christmas specials right now. Buy two off that rack there, and get a third shirt for free."

"Thanks," he said, aware his tone was still far too curt. "I need to get home, but I'll be back."

"The special lasts until Friday."

"Good to know. Thanks."

Sam fumed the whole drive home.

Ivy had changed. She'd always been an open book before, but she was all shuttered up now. Outwardly, she might still be the beautiful Ivy he knew, but there was a new guard up, a new hardness he didn't recognize. He didn't know what to think of the change, didn't know what to think of her working at a stripper bar, either. Ivy was no prude, but she was a nice girl, conservative, raised in the church. She didn't mess around. She didn't take unnecessary risks. She lived for her horses and competing. But losing her mom two years ago had rocked her world. Ivy and her mom, Shelby, had been close, practically best friends, but then Ivy seemed to bounce back quickly, moving on with new boyfriend Wes, getting bigger sponsors, and a lot more visibility. Suddenly she was in magazines, featured in Instagram stories and ads. Slender, beautiful, photogenic, everybody wanted her, and she should have made a lot of money on those national sponsors.

So, if she'd made those lucrative deals, why was she scraping by here in Marietta? And why had she been reduced to working at the Wolf Den?

Something didn't add up, and Sam didn't know what bothered him more—the fact that he was so upset to see her there, or the fact she didn't even seem to care that he'd come looking for her.

It wasn't his problem, he told himself. Ivy was an adult, free to do whatever she wanted. But at the same time, Sam had promised her mom that he'd look out for her, and so far he'd done a pretty poor job of it.

Sam growled deep in his throat, foot heavy on the accelerator, as if he could outrun the vision of her in his head, in her tight red T-shirt and even tighter, fitted jeans, her western belt with the big silver buckle flat against her narrow waist, smiling at the bikers, calling them *boys*.

Those bikers weren't boys. And back when they were together, Ivy didn't know how to make a drink. Heck, she didn't even drink. So why was she working the bar at the Wolf Den?

IVY EXHALED HARD after Sam left. That had been weird. And incredibly uncomfortable. She didn't like discussing Wes, and she certainly didn't feel as if she had to defend herself to Sam, of all people. Sam Wyatt with his lofty plans and ambitions. Sam, with his dreams so big there wasn't room for anyone else but him.

And then Ivy kicked herself, because she wasn't being fair. Not totally.

Sam had never been bad to her. He just hadn't given her enough.

She'd loved him, too, loved him so much it made her heart ache, but in the end, he'd let her go and that... well, that had broken her heart.

So, no, she didn't hate him. How could you hate beautiful, swaggering, immensely talented Sam Wyatt? The cowboy was so confident, so intense, he reminded her of the sun. Necessary. Brilliant.

Scorching.

The scorching part was why she'd broken up with him. There just didn't seem to be room enough in his sphere for both of them, and the only way for her heart to survive was for her to put space between them.

And yet, she'd hoped he'd come after her. She prayed he'd realize how much he missed her. But there was no epiphany on his part. He'd taken her at her word and moved forward with his life and career without her.

Sam's single-minded focus was what made him so successful on the rodeo circuit. But that same single-minded focus made him a terrible boyfriend. She'd known from the beginning he was competitive and driven. He didn't like turning down opportunities or events or money, not even so his brothers—or Ivy—could succeed. Initially, she hadn't minded. She'd been an only child and she was plenty independent. Ivy figured out how to succeed around him, carving space out for herself so she could focus on her own events. It was only as time went on, and they were getting more serious, that she came to resent how Sam always came first and she came last. Why should it be her compromising all the time? Why didn't he compromise more?

Maybe the problem was that she and Sam were too much alike. They both wanted big things, and neither were willing to make the necessary concessions a relationship needed. They'd always had a passionate relationship. When things were good it was very, very good, but when things weren't good, it was very, very bad.

After the breakup, Ivy waited and waited to hear from him. Waited and waited for an olive branch. The waiting made her angry. They'd had so much history together. So much love. But Sam seemed to have forgotten the love, and after four brutal, lonely months—months where she cried every single day, if not twice a day—she realized he wasn't coming back for her. There would be no reconciliation. They were done.

Through.

Then, in the middle of that year of that heartbreak, her mom died, and grieving for Sam was swallowed into grief over losing the most inspiring person Ivy knew. Ivy's mom had been a trailblazer and fearless. A six-time national barrel racing champion, Ivy's mom, Shelby Lynn, did the impossible, and she did it with style and grit and courage.

*Courage.*

Ivy tried to cling to some of that same courage as she made funeral arrangements for her mom and then decisions of what to do with her mom's estate. Sam sent flowers with a card that read, *Thinking of you. So very sorry for your loss. Sam.*

That was all the card said.

That was all Sam could think of saying to her after so many months?

Ivy cried holding the card, crying hard because she realized that this was the best Sam could do, or would do, and it simply wasn't enough.

His attempt to be sympathetic was pitiful.

She rejected it, and him, throwing away the card, and then the next day, throwing out the flowers because it hurt her, just seeing them. Better to not see them. Better to not be reminded of him.

Wes, a stock supplier who she'd known from the rodeo, sent flowers, too. She kept those flowers. She didn't know Wes well, but his flowers were beautiful and they gave her no pain. He called a week later to see if she needed anything. She said she didn't but thank you. He called two weeks later, letting her know he was in the area, and would she want to meet for coffee or a drink? Ivy thought about the invitation for a couple of hours, then texted that yes she'd enjoy meeting him, and the rest was history.

Bad history.

# Chapter Two

S AM COULD FEEL his mother's gaze all afternoon. She'd watched him during their late lunch—he'd made her a turkey bacon sandwich, her favorite—and every time there was a lull in the conversation, and he thought she'd ask him something personal, he dove into another story about Las Vegas, or his horses, or his shoulder, and whether he should get surgery or not.

He managed to escape the kitchen before she brought up whatever was on her mind, but now as they sat down at the dinner table, he could feel her watching him again, her brows slightly flattened, mouth firm, as she gazed at him from her place at the foot of the table.

If he could have headed to town and gotten a burger and beer at Grey's Saloon, he would. But you didn't do that to Mom, not so soon after returning from a lengthy absence.

During dinner, he tuned out the laughter and bantering. Tommy and Billy were like two kids, always having a good time together. Joe was smitten with his bride, unable to even eat without looking at her and smiling crookedly.

Joe being happy changed the house. Or maybe it was

Sophie's happiness. But the Wyatt Ranch felt warm and bright and full of love. It was almost too much love.

Even as a boy, Sam had found the noise overwhelming at times. He was more introverted than his brothers, and required a lot of alone time, something that was hard to find on the ranch, especially when everyone was home.

As his mom's concerned gaze met his, Sam forced a smile. He wasn't going to have her worry. There was no reason to worry.

His mom wasn't buying it, though, but she did eventually look away, and nod and then respond to something Sophie was saying. His mom liked Sophie. And his grandad, well Grandad treated Sophie like a princess, or more accurately, the granddaughter he'd never had.

After the blessing was said and huge platters were passed around, Sam's thoughts returned to Ivy, and suddenly he wasn't interested in eating.

Ivy had struggled with his need for space. She didn't understand why he'd pull away, or want to go for a drive on his own. She always wanted to go with him, always eager to keep him company, and he hated hurting her feelings, but he couldn't unwind or recharge with others. It wasn't her that he wanted to escape, it was everyone. Unfortunately, she took it personally, which turned into arguments neither of them needed.

Thinking of Ivy made Sam's chest tighten.

They'd had a messy breakup. She'd said hard things

when she ended the relationship, and he'd been hurt and refused to think of her, refused to miss her. But when he'd discovered Ivy's mom, Shelby, wasn't well, he did what he could to ease her suffering.

Shelby had made him promise to look after Ivy, and he'd made the promise, fully intending to keep it. But after Shelby was gone and Ivy was dating Wes, Ivy wouldn't talk to Sam. In fact, she wanted nothing to do with him. Wes more or less said so to his face. Sam had longed to smash his fist into Wes's stupid, smug face, but he didn't. Instead, Sam kept his distance, making sure to avoid Wes and Ivy. They were not his favorite people, and they were most definitely not his favorite couple.

Dinner over, Sam rose to clear the table, indicating his desire to do the dishes. He had offers from the others to help, but he refused, preferring to clean up on his own. He scraped and filled up the sink, staring at the basin as it filled with hot sudsy water, doing his best not to think or remember more than necessary. Ivy wasn't his problem. Ivy wasn't his girlfriend. Ivy—

"So tell me about Ivy," his mom said, her voice coming from behind him.

Sam stiffened at his mother's question, not realizing she was there in the kitchen with him, nor how long she'd been standing there watching him. Ivy was exactly what he didn't want to discuss, but at the same time, he'd never be rude to his mom. Sam turned the faucet off and then pivoted to look at his mother, who was standing next to the kitchen table, leaning on her cane. "Aren't you missing the news?" he asked, familiar with his mother's routine. Every night after dinner, Mom and Grandad would watch the news. Half hour local, followed by a half hour national.

"It's the same old news from this morning," his mom answered, carefully drawing a chair out and even more carefully sitting down. "Fortunately, or unfortunately, depending on whether you're a news anchor."

He smiled faintly. He liked his mom. She'd been through a lot and she was still here, ruling the roost. "I'm not sure what you know, or what Tommy has told you, but she's working in town, bartending."

"At the Wolf Den."

So Tommy had said a lot.

Sam suppressed a wave of irritation. "Yeah."

"That's got to worry you. It's not an Ivy kind of place."

His mom had met Ivy over the years, and while Sam wouldn't say Ivy and his mom were close, they'd gotten along well. His mom had even met Ivy's mom, Shelby Lynn, when he and Ivy were serious, when he thought maybe, just maybe, he'd propose. "She's a big girl. She knows what she's doing."

"What brought her to Crawford County?"

"She got an offer to work on the Kruse Ranch here. But the job didn't pan out."

"What about her horses? Where are they?"

Trust his mom to remember the thing most important to Ivy. Ivy loved her mares. They were everything to her. "I'm sure she's found a place for them. They might even be up on the Kruse Ranch still. It would make sense to board them there."

"You didn't ask?"

"Didn't cross my mind."

Summer eyed him steadily. No judgment in her expression, just an awareness that made Sam uneasy. He and his mom might not talk all that much, but she understood him pretty well, recognizing he might keep things close to his chest, but he felt deeply and was loyal to a fault. "Had to be a shock seeing her, though. It's been a while, hasn't it?"

"I think the last time I saw her was in Calgary, last July at the Stampede."

"Was her boyfriend up there? That Wesley guy?"

Sam fought the urge to smile. His mom knew more than he'd imagined. "Yeah, Wes was around. I'm not a big fan of him, so I steered clear."

"Why don't you like him?"

"He's an ass. But I'm not the one dating him, so it doesn't matter what I think."

"Is Ivy still dating him?"

"No. I don't think so."

"What happened?"

Sam gave her an incredulous look. "*Mom.*"

Her eyes widened, managing to make her look both innocent and indignant at the same time. "I thought you talked to her today. Sorry, my bad." She slowly pushed up from the kitchen table and reached for her cane. "You've got dishes to do. I better let you get them done." And then she walked out.

But after his mom left, Sam felt worse.

He could hear his brothers in the family room talking and joking, could hear Sophie's laugh, and Sam could picture Joe's smile. Joe was amused by his wife, and admired her for holding her own with his rambunctious younger brothers.

And just like that, Sam thought of Ivy, remembering how close she'd been with Tommy and Billy. The four of them traveled a lot together, Ivy and Sam in his rig, with Tommy and Billy in theirs, but almost every morning they had coffee together, and almost every night they had dinner somewhere. They were their own family on the road, and Ivy had been—

Sam stopped himself there, teeth gritted, chest tight.

He didn't want to keep thinking about her. He didn't want to feel this hot tangled emotion. She wasn't his anymore. She hadn't been his for two and a half years.

After Ivy broke up with him, Sam didn't date anyone for a year. He hadn't been interested in seeing anyone, or even getting physical, but then Tommy asked Sam to play wingman, telling him he was needed, that he couldn't ignore his brother. Tommy did just fine on his own, and could have easily handled a date with two women, but Sam had agreed and showered and shaved and put on clean jeans and an ironed shirt and had gone out.

The date had taken place in Sioux City, and the girl had been a sweet young Midwestern thing, with long golden curls, big blue eyes, deep dimples. Sam didn't know if she was innocent, silly, or both, but she laughed at every single thing Sam said. It hadn't been the worst date he'd ever been on, but after giving her a kiss good night, he knew he would never see her again. There was no need to see her again. She wasn't his type and he most definitely had a type. He liked slim, fine-boned girls with long brown hair, hazel-green eyes, girls that could ride a horse better than a man.

Ivy had been his type. Ivy had been his girl. But she'd wanted something else, something more, and he did what he had to do—set her free.

IVY WOKE UP to the sound of Joan, her landlady, talking loudly on the phone in the hallway outside her bedroom door, her conversation peppered with colorful curses.

Ivy glanced at the bedside clock. It wasn't even seven yet and she'd gone to bed well past midnight. She pulled her pillow over her head, trying to block out Joan's voice. But sleep didn't come, not even after Joan's voice finally, thankfully faded. After another fifteen minutes of silently grumbling, Ivy threw back the covers, slid a heavy robe over her pajamas and headed to the kitchen for coffee.

But the coffeepot was off, cold and empty, and when Ivy checked the big red coffee canister, that was empty as well. She'd just bought ground coffee a few days ago. How could it be gone already? But she knew the answer. Chain-smoking Joan, alternated her cigarettes with endless cups of coffee. From now on, Ivy would have to keep some emergency coffee hidden somewhere.

Back in her room, Ivy dressed quickly, sliding her feet into socks and then her fleece-lined snow boots to make the walk to Java Café on Main Street. Joan was on the front porch, when Ivy stepped outside, smoking a cigarette even as she shouted another four-letter swear word into the phone.

Joan nodded grimly at her. Ivy lifted a hand in return and made her way down the icy walkway to the street. There was no sidewalk at this end of Chance Avenue, and she walked along the asphalt, following the railroad tracks, the cold, fresh winter air clearing her head, while the brisk wind made her eyes water and cheeks sting.

She walked, lost in thought, until she crossed the tracks, passed the handsome depot, and a block later, reached the Graff Hotel. Ivy paused a moment to admire the old hotel. The four-story red brick Graff looked festive with its greenery and wreaths on the front door. A smart-looking bell captain stood on the hotel's front steps, ready to help any guests coming or going. She'd never been inside but it was on her to-do list. She'd heard they had an enormous Christmas tree in the lobby and gingerbread houses on display.

She felt a pang as she thought of Christmas. It was true she wasn't looking forward to the holiday this year, but it hadn't always been the case. Growing up, she and her mom had their own traditions. They bought and delivered dozens of dinners for the less fortunate in Custer—hams and turkeys, stuffing, potatoes, gravy, rolls and pies—and made roll-out sugar cookies and Mom's amazing pumpkin bread. Because it was just the two of them, Christmas wasn't fancy, but it was heartfelt. Christmas morning meant Ivy's stocking and homemade waffles, then church, hymns and carols, and once back home, opening the few gifts under the tree and dinner.

Mom didn't have a great voice, but oh, how she loved to sing. And she'd practically belt out her favorite carols like "Joy to the World," as she cooked or washed or folded laundry.

Ivy tugged on her mittens, somewhat wistful, very nostalgic, and continued on to Java Café. Often she just got a coffee to go. This morning, she ordered coffee and a breakfast burrito and sat at one of the small tables in the corner and scrolled through the news on her phone while waiting for her breakfast to be prepared. The news always left her feeling so flattened she wasn't sure why she bothered.

It was a relief when her name was called and she collected her burrito from the counter and was on her way back to her table when she spotted a man that looked familiar. It took her a moment to place him, then realized it was Ian Wallace, the man who'd bought Belle for his daughter. Her heart swooshed so hard she felt almost sick. Pulse racing, she stopped at his table to say hello.

He glanced up, puzzled, and then his expression cleared. "Ivy Wyckoff."

She had to force a smile and remind herself he wasn't the enemy. It had been her choice to sell the mare. He hadn't kidnapped Belle. Ivy had willingly sold her horse to help Ashley. "How's Belle?"

"She's doing okay."

She frowned. "Problems?"

"It's been a bumpier start than we thought, but of course, there is always an adjustment when a horse has a new jockey."

Ivy's insides lurched again. Belle was as steady as they came. "Is your daughter having a hard time?"

"You didn't tell me the mare is a little headstrong, but I suppose she'll settle in once she realizes she's stuck with us, and we're her home now."

Ivy hated his answer. She exhaled hard, finding it difficult to speak. "If there's something I can do… Happy to work with your daughter and Belle—"

"That's not necessary. Let's not confuse the horse. You're out of the picture now. Lizzie's in charge. The horse will learn that soon enough. Head of the herd, right?"

Ivy managed the briefest of nods before moving on. She

understood Belle wasn't hers anymore, but it crushed her to know that Belle wasn't adjusting well to her new home.

Ivy stuffed the hot breakfast burrito into her pocket and asked for a to-go cup for her coffee and headed outside, needing to put distance between her and Ian Wallace.

Ian had paid top dollar for Belle and Ivy was sure the mare wouldn't be treated badly, but still, Ivy felt terrible. She wished she hadn't bumped into Ian Wallace at all.

Ivy walked down a block and leaned against the old bank, which was now a popular upscale steakhouse but only opened for dinner, and ate her burrito there, letting the sun warm her and melt some of the ice around her heart.

It had been hard handing Belle over. Four months had passed since she'd driven Belle to the Wallace property and backed her out of the trailer. Lizzie Wallace was an eleven-year-old tomboy, skinny, freckled face and very blonde. She was also unbelievably excited to have a horse like Belle as her own. Lizzie had begun to compete, and although she was still pretty new at it, she had a fearlessness that boded well for the sport.

It had been easy leaving Belle, believing Belle would be in great hands.

Now Ivy worried Belle's new home wasn't a good fit, and that was tough, because Belle was like family to her.

Belle had a heart of gold. She loved to win, but even more than that, she lived to make Ivy happy. Together, they'd won a lot of titles, and some really big money.

Together they had been one of the best teams in barrel racing.

Ivy crumpled the remaining burrito in the foil wrapped and tossed it away.

She had to remember why she'd sold Belle, that there had been a reason for the transaction. Selling Belle had allowed Ivy to do something huge. Something life changing. There were more important things than being a nationally ranked barrel racer, and more important things than making the WPRA's World Finals Rodeo in November, or the PRCA's National Finals Rodeo in December.

There was going to school.

There were dances, dates, and falling in love.

There was independence.

Ashley deserved a shot at a normal life, and if selling Belle meant that Ashley could get the right physical and occupational therapy at one of the best rehab programs in the country for spinal cord injured adolescents, then Ivy had made the right decision.

Even if it had been a little impulsive.

Thank goodness her mom wasn't around to know. Her mom was the complete opposite—grounded, focused, practical, tenacious. She'd had a plan for everything, and she stuck to her plans, never changing them just because she got a new idea. Whims were ignored. Emotion was managed. And impulse firmly reined in.

Ivy sighed inwardly. No, she was most definitely not like

her mom.

On her way back to the house, she stopped by the garage to see if her truck was still there. It was. She let the mechanic know she should have the rest of the money soon to get the transmission fixed. "Hopefully before Christmas. Maybe in the next few days?" she said.

He assured her that he had the part and was ready to go and Ivy thanked him, before walking back to the house. She pulled out her hatbox where she was stashing her cash and counted it up again. Two thousand six hundred. Two more good nights and she should have what she needed for the repair. Another month and she might have enough to put a couple thousand down on a place, not to buy, of course, but to lease, and when she did that, she'd get Scotch from Kruse ranch, and she'd be able to ride again, and train again, and maybe even compete again. That was the piece she hadn't yet figured out. Once, she'd loved barrel racing, but with Mom gone, and Wes interfering so much in her career, she'd lost the fire. Ivy couldn't even imagine entering any events next month—and to be honest, she wouldn't do well, not without Belle. Scotch showed promise, but he was still young, and he didn't have Belle's heart.

Eyes burning, throat aching, Ivy exhaled and lay back on her bed, covering her face with her forearm. Her eyes burned and a lump filled her throat. She didn't know if it was seeing Sam yesterday, or bumping into Ian Wallace at the Java Café, but Ivy suddenly missed her old life. Her mom. Belle.

The ranch she'd been raised on in Custer. It had been a good life, but she'd been too young, too blind, and too ambitious, to know it.

Where had it all gone wrong? It started with the breakup with Sam, and then she'd failed by not being with Mom while she was dying, and then rebounding with Wes, who wasn't a prince but a wolf in cowboy boots and a hat. The moment Ivy realized Wes was bad news, she should have kicked him out of her life. Instead, the wolf took over her business affairs, her calendar, her decisions, until little by little he stole even the oxygen she breathed.

It took a hard fall in August to face the fact that she was miserable, and weeks later, when Ivy heard about Ashley, Ivy knew what she had to do. Start over. Be brave. Do something good for someone else. And so she did. She quit barrel racing, sold Belle, and got a job far from the competitive world she'd known.

The changes had been scary and overwhelming, but also liberating. Wes didn't know where she was. She felt free for the first time in a year. She was determined to live differently in the future. No regrets. No going back. No self-pity, either.

No self-pity, she reminded herself, sitting up and putting the hatbox filled with cash away. Head to the shared bathroom down the hall where she showered and washed her hair, before blowing it dry.

Back in her room, she dressed for work in fresh jeans and a fitted T-shirt. Wolf Den owner, George, liked her to keep things tight and so she did. The customers liked it, and they liked it even better when she was friendly, so she kept them happy and was rewarded with very generous tips.

Arriving at work, Ivy winced as she entered the bar, music blaring from the overhead speakers. She didn't mind rock music, but every now and then, the heavy-metal cocktail waitress, Lucy, preferred put Ivy's teeth on edge. And today, the Christmas decorations at the Wolf Den looked even more pathetic than usual, lending a sad, tawdry nostalgia to the bar.

Tattered silver garland hung above the bar itself while another silver garland swag was taped beneath the counter. A couple cheap plastic wreaths dotted the interior, wreaths that were boxed up and pulled out every year. A white plastic banner reading *Ho Ho Ho* was thumbtacked above one door, and a three-foot-tall illuminated Santa had been squeezed in between all the liquor bottles.

Ivy patted the plastic Santa's belly and then turned the music down a notch. She'd just stepped away from the stereo, when she heard a stool scrape the floor of the bar.

Turning, Ivy spotted a woman about her age standing on the other side of the counter, the woman's straight hair, black, or nearly black, fell to her butt.

"Can I help you?" Ivy asked.

"Yes, please. A Diet Coke with a twist of lime if you have lime; otherwise just Diet Coke is fine."

Ivy slowly reached for a glass, keeping her gaze fixed on

the stranger. "You a cop?" she asked bluntly.

The woman laughed. "No, do I look like a cop?"

"FBI?"

The woman laughed again. "No. But you kind of make me want to be. Sounds interesting." The woman held out her hand. "I'm Sophie Wyatt. Married to Joe Wyatt. I thought I'd stop by and introduce myself. Figured it might be nice to know a girl around here."

Ivy's lips slowly curved. "So you're Joe's wife. Congratulations. You got one of the good ones."

Sophie grinned, her expression mischievous. "Are there bad Wyatt's?"

Now it was Ivy's turn to laugh. "No, not talking about the Wyatt's, although that's funny. I just meant Joe is solid. He's… honest. True."

Sophie's smile faded. "Sounds like you and Sam ended on bad terms."

"Relationships end because they're not working. Ours stopped working. Not a victim and he's not a victim. It just… ended. I have nothing bad to say about him, and hopefully he has nothing bad to say about me."

"I've only heard great things about you. Maybe that's why I'm here; just felt like maybe you could use the phone number of someone that wasn't a Wyatt brother. Just in case you ever needed it. But you probably have a lot of friends here—"

"No. No, I don't have a lot of friends here. Working at

the Wolf Den doesn't exactly build your circle of friendship, but I've become friendly with some of the waitresses. Pia. Lucy. They're nice, and they look out for me."

"I'm glad you're not all on your own then." Sophie hesitated. "Are you joining either of them for Christmas? Feel like Christmas with us?"

"At the Wyatt's?"

"It's my home now, too."

Ivy shrugged uneasily. "I'm working Christmas."

"I'm sure you either have the morning or evening off."

"I don't think that would be a good idea. Even though Sam and I aren't enemies, we're not exactly… close. It would be uncomfortable for both of us spending Christmas together."

"Well, if you change your mind, I'd love to have you there. Even better, maybe one day we could meet up for lunch? I work here in town, just six or seven blocks over, at the Wright Salon. I run the front desk and help with bookkeeping and ordering things. It was supposed to be a temporary job when I moved here last spring but I like it, and I like Mandy and all the girls. It's nice to be around women."

Ivy smiled reluctantly. "There is a lot testosterone at the Wyatt Ranch."

"You can say that again. Most of the time it's good, but every now and then, well, it's a whole lot of a lot." She glanced at her watch, grimaced, and then reached into her coat pocket, retrieving a glossy pink business card. "Speaking of work, I better go, but here's the number of the salon, and my cell number, too. Let's get lunch, and please, feel free to call me anytime."

Ivy watched the door a moment as it closed behind Sophie.

Joe was married. And married to a really wonderful woman. Ivy was happy for him. But she felt a little pang because, once upon a time, when she and Sam had been together, the Wyatt brothers used to tease, placing bets that Sam would be the first Wyatt to marry. And once upon a time, she'd been sure of it, too.

Ivy came from behind the counter to adjust the barstools, lining them up just so. The Wolf Den might be a dark, dingy bar with the worst reputation in town, but she could at least make sure it was tidy and clean when she started her shift.

An hour later, Sam arrived. Ivy had been surprised when he'd appeared yesterday, but was even more shocked that he'd returned today.

She watched as he peeled off his heavy leather jacket and drape it over the back of his barstool before sitting down, just one seat from where Sophie had been sitting earlier.

Her heart gave a double beat, and she felt a sudden surge of adrenaline that made her legs feel wobbly. "Hello, Sam."

"Hello, Ivy." He removed his hat, and ran a hand through his dark blond hair. Some men were pretty as young males, and others just got better looking as they matured. Sam was one of those that just got more rugged and more physically appealing with time.

"What brings you back?" she asked. "Because I know it's not me."

"Hoping for another free beer. You know I love a good deal."

The corner of her mouth lifted. The idea of Sam, with all his money, and all of his big endorsements, needing a free beer made her want to laugh. But it also made her chest squeeze tight. Weird, seeing him here two days in a row. Weird remembering just how much she loved him. "Want anything with that beer? A lot of folks love the hot dogs. We also have nachos. They're both hot and fresh right now. Can't promise you they'll be the same tonight."

"As delicious as those both sound, I think I'll just stick with a glass of water. No ice."

"Demanding, aren't you?"

"That's what I've been told."

Her heart slammed into her chest and her cheeks burned hot, even as she went cold, aware she was the one who'd called him demanding. She was the one who said he was selfish. She'd tossed all that at him and more the day she'd broken up with him.

She filled a glass with water and pushed it across the counter to him. "Everyone home for Christmas?" she asked, anxious to change the subject.

"Yep."

"Your mom likes Christmas, doesn't she?"

"Her birthday is the twenty-third so we all make an effort to come home for Christmas. Makes her happy to have those three days with us. And Marietta is festive, too. Everyone seems like they're always in a good mood."

"I noticed that during the Stroll. You would have thought we were straight out of a movie set."

Sam laughed, low and husky. "Marietta thinks it's Disneyland once Main Street is all dressed up for the holidays."

"Has it always been this way?"

"Ever since I was a kid. Marietta has a lot of pride. She's a good little town; always wants everyone to be happy."

"Marietta is a girl?"

"I call her a girl. She's pretty, smart, and tough… determined to be independent. Heck, sounds like I'm describing you, Ivy."

The heat returned to her face. She reached over the counter to take a drink order from Lucy. "Not that tough," she said, scanning the list of cocktails and beer. She looked up at Sam, her gaze meeting his. "Not that independent, either. Not even that successful."

"You were doing really well this year on the circuit. And even better last year."

"I don't know if my heart's in it anymore. I'm beginning to wonder if I'm done."

"I might not be your boyfriend anymore, but I'm still

your friend. Why don't you tell me what's going on?"

"What makes you think anything is going on?"

"Ivy, you're working at a bar in the middle of Crawford County. You're pouring booze instead of training horses. And from what Billy told me, you're renting a room from a pill poppin' old lady—"

"She's not that old. And how did Billy know?"

"It's a small town, easy to ask some questions."

Ivy glanced at the door as it opened and closed. A group of young cowboys entered, talking and laughing, sounding as if they'd already had a few drinks somewhere else. "You might have been raised here, but you don't own this town, and you don't own me—"

"Never said I did." Sam's blue gaze locked with hers. "Can't even imagine you have your horses with you."

She counted to five, and then ten. "I don't," she said shortly, hating the confession.

Now Sam looked as pissed off as she felt. "You should be someplace better. You should be—" He broke off, shook his head.

Ivy leaned on the counter, leaning into his space. "Where should I be, Sam? Where should I call home? Mom's gone and she was the only family I had."

"Your dad's not dead," Sam said gruffly.

"And you know he's not interested in being in my life, or he wouldn't have walked out when I was four."

"Have you tried to reach out to him?"

"For what?"

"I don't know. That's for you two to find out."

"Sam, he sent a fruit basket when he heard Mom died." She grabbed a sponge, wiped down the wet sink and squeezed the excess water out, thinking that it might have been two years since she and Sam truly talked, but they were right back where they used to be. Arguing. "If that's his idea of comfort, I'm good on my own."

"Are you good on your own?" Sam's voice sounded hard and dry. "You keep saying you are, but sweetheart, I don't believe you."

She felt a spike of pain at his words but she smothered it. "Your problem, not mine."

Silence stretched. Sam's gaze never wavered from her face, making her feel hot and prickly all over. Making her feel, which wasn't good, because feelings were dangerous, and emotions were her downfall.

"Can't we keep it cordial?" he said quietly.

She ignored the sting of tears at the back of her eyes. "Hard to be cordial when you're judging me."

He shrugged, his big shoulders rolling beneath the snug fit of his granite-colored Henley. "Not judging. Just trying to catch up."

She didn't trust his smile because it didn't even warm his eyes, and right now his blue eyes looked glacier cold. He was pissed off and she could feel his fury from across the bar counter. "You're rattling me, cowboy." She struggled to smile. "How can I pour drinks when my hands are shaking?"

"Can't have that. I didn't come here to upset you."

"Good, because I won't like seeing you walk in this place if you're just coming to give me grief."

He laughed, creases fanning from his eyes. "Well, let's change the conversation then because I want you happy when you see me."

"Hmmm." Ivy's brows arched. "So how did you do at the NFRs this year?" she asked, because the Wyatt's were always going to the national finals, and it was as safe a topic as she could think of.

"I did okay," he said.

It was a big deal for her to qualify for Vegas, but Tommy, Billy, and Sam were regulars. She couldn't think of a time when they hadn't made the top fifteen in the last four years.

"Just how good was 'okay'?"

"Took third in steer wrestling."

"Good job. That's some nice money."

He hesitated. "And first in tie-down roping."

Her jaw dropped slightly. Sam had come close to first, but had never taken a first before. "World champion, huh?"

He nodded modestly. "Yep."

"That's got to feel good."

"I'm pretty happy."

"How about Tommy and Billy? Did they both go?"

"They did well but I did the best this year. 'Bout time,

too. Frustrating when your little brothers kicked your butt."

She smiled, picturing his brothers. Tommy and Billy were fun and funny. They'd had so many good times together. "It must be awfully frustrating for the rest of the cowboys that there are three of you competing. Everyone's probably praying the Wyatt's retire."

"Tommy and Billy are nowhere near retirement. I've begun to consider it, but not ready yet. Maybe in another three or four years. We'll see how the body holds up."

"Shoulder?" she guessed.

He nodded.

She bent down, grabbed a bottle of beer from the refrigerator and cracking the cap, pushed the bottle toward him. "Still putting off surgery?"

He nodded again.

"Why don't you just do the surgery?" she asked, hands on her hips.

His mouth quirked. "Now you sound just like my mom."

"I'll take that as a compliment."

The corner of his lips lifted higher. "I guess that is."

She raised a hand, gesturing to one of the regulars entering the bar. This one had a soft spot for Lucy so she wouldn't have to do anything until Lucy came with his drink order. "So how long are you home this time?"

"Only until Christmas. I leave early the day after. Have some business to take care of in Cody."

"Who does business the day after Christmas?"

"A seller anxious to close a deal."

"Are you buying or selling?"

"I'm buying," he said.

"What are you buying?"

"Property."

Her eyebrow arched. "In Wyoming?"

He nodded.

"What kind of property?"

"What do you think, Ivy?" he countered, sounding exasperated.

She flashed him a sharp look before heading down the bar to make the rum and Coke Lucy's customer always ordered. Easy on the cola, heavy on the rum. And this time she took an extra-long time to make the cocktail to give herself time to calm down.

Sam was buying a ranch, in Wyoming, when his family had a huge ranch, right here, adjacent to Crawford County. Why would he do that? Didn't he care that he had the best family in the world right here? A family that loved him and supported him no matter what?

Ivy would have given anything to have a family like his, and Sam just took it for granted.

SAM LIFTED THE icy beer bottle to his mouth but drank almost nothing. Instead, he watched Ivy down at the end of the bar, talking up a storm with a red-haired cocktail waitress with dangly earrings and a very short black skirt. Ivy was annoyed with him and that was fine. He was plenty annoyed with her. She was the one who walked away from him, from *them*, and the dreams they'd once shared. As a single man he could do what he wanted, and he was doing just that, creating the best possible life for himself.

A moment later she sauntered back to where he was sitting, her long ponytail slipping over her collarbone, a wash of pink on her cheeks. "You're buying a ranch," she said, her tone sharp, even as she gave him a look he didn't much like.

"It's good land, a lot of acres, perfect for cattle and some crops."

"In Wyoming," she added disdainfully.

"Three hours from here. Not the end of the world."

"What did your family say?"

"Haven't told everyone yet."

She gave him a long, pointed stare. "You're going to upset them. And you're doing this at Christmas."

"They've all known for years that I have no desire to live forever in Pray. I love Paradise Valley, but it's not home."

"Yes, it is home. You're back home right now."

"I'm a Wyatt, whether or not I live on the ranch."

She nodded to a group of men entering the bar, her smile faint, tight, before turning back to him. "You couldn't find anything closer?"

"I wanted something central, so that I could use the place

as a home base between rodeos. It's under thirteen hours from Cody to Vegas—"

"That's what it is from Marietta, too, so don't use that as an excuse."

"Maybe I just want to get away from everyone."

She eyed him a long time, jaw tight. "That's why we didn't work. Every time I wanted to be with you, you just wanted to escape."

"We spent plenty of time together," he said gruffly.

"Oh, right. In your truck, driving across the country. In the rig, jammed into the bunk."

He eyed her for a long moment, not interested in continuing that conversation. "So when did you wrap up your year? I saw you in Calgary in July, but then you seemed to have disappeared."

"I wrapped up toward the end of August when it became clear I wouldn't be qualifying for Vegas this year."

"I suppose you have enough sponsors you can afford to do that."

Her mouth opened, closed. "Yeah," she said after a moment, her gaze dropping to the counter where she rubbed halfheartedly at a scratch.

There was nothing convincing about that answer. He waited a moment, swigged his beer, and set the bottle down. "You still enjoying competing?"

She shrugged. "It's not… I'm not…"

Her voice faded but he didn't try to fill the silence. He

wanted to hear what she had to say.

It took her a moment but she finally answered. "It's not the same, Sam, not since Mom died. She loved the sport. Horses and competing were her passion." Ivy's fine dark eyebrows flattened. "I'm beginning to realize they might not be mine."

"Horses or competition? Because those are two different things."

She glanced at him, caught off guard.

He nodded. "You can love one without the other, and let's face it; we both know you can't live without your horses. They're everything to you."

"That's true. I'm not over horses. I want to train them. I want to continue what Mom started. But I can't do that without having a place of my own, but I'm working toward it. That's the big goal."

"You have your mom's place in Custer. Why not go there?"

"I've leased it out. It's a five-year lease, and even if I wanted to break it, I couldn't. I know, because I consulted a real estate attorney for advice."

"But you could use the money coming in from that place to pay for another place."

"Theoretically, yes."

It was obvious she didn't want to tell him everything. "I'm not following."

"The point is, I'm not giving up on horses. I just don't know that I'll be competing anytime again soon."

"Belle's not going to like that. She gets depressed when you don't take her out to turn and burn around those barrels."

"She's still running. Just not with me on her back."

"*What?*"

Ivy couldn't, or wouldn't, look at him. "I sold her."

"But how? Why?"

"I…" Her voice faded. She swallowed and tried again. "I… oh, it's hard to explain."

"Try me."

"It's complicated."

"I'm listening."

"I saw an opportunity where I could help someone, and so I did."

"By selling your mother's horse?"

"She's *my* horse. Was my horse."

"As well as the daughter of your mother's champion Trixie. Bred by your mom. Raised by your mom—"

"*I* raised her," Ivy interrupted fiercely. "With Mom, yes, but she was mine."

For the second time in days, he saw red. Ivy was killing him. This was madness. Belle was the perfect horse for Ivy, a talented mare, a champion mare with impeccable bloodlines. And not to be melodramatic, but Belle was as close to family as Ivy had. "But why Belle? Why not Scotch? He'd get you more money."

"He hurt his leg in August. We took a fall together. I couldn't get full value from him, and who wants to buy a horse that might go lame?"

"He's not lame."

"Not now, no, because I took care of him, but if I'd sold him to someone who didn't know horses or wouldn't take his time getting Scotch back in condition—" She broke off, lifted her chin, refusing to be cowed. "Fortunately, he's good now."

"Only you lost Belle."

Her confidence began to fail. "Let's not talk about it."

"This is *Belle* we're discussing."

"I *know*, Sam. And there are days that it just slays me that I sold her, but I had my reasons for selling her, and I still believe I did the right thing."

"Who bought her?"

"A local rancher named Ian Wallace. His daughter Lizzie takes lessons up at Kruse Ranch. That's where I met Lizzie. She was just starting to get into barrel racing, and Ian was eager for her to compete on a winner."

"A junior barrel racer doesn't need one of the best barrel racing horses in the country."

"He paid me well for her."

"How well?"

"That's none of your business."

Sam couldn't hide his disgust. "I don't even know who you are anymore."

"Great. That makes two of us," she answered, before walking away.

# CHAPTER THREE

A T THE WYATT Ranch, the whole family was smashed into the small paneled TV room watching a Christmas movie, a tradition his mother had started when they were little, and a tradition they continued for her each year because it made her happy. Every night a different member of the family would pick a holiday movie. Tonight it was *Christmas Vacation*, Billy's pick, and the family was enjoying it, but Sam couldn't relax, and he kept getting up to get a drink of water, and step outside to get some air.

The dogs came bounding from the barn, and Sam gave each of the three a pat. They circled around him a moment, deciding if they wanted to stay or return to where it was warm. Runt decided to stay while Penny and Duke headed back to the barn. Sam didn't blame them. It was freezing, and snow was imminent, but the icy air felt better than the stuffy family room filled with too many bodies, even though they were bodies he loved.

He was still outside when the movie finished. Billy stuck his head out the door to tell him, adding that Joe sucked, and he hadn't followed the 'rules.' The rules of Christmas movie night were that they stayed together, and watched the movies together, but Sam didn't care, and was glad when Billy closed the door.

Moments later the door opened again and he waited for Tommy to appear, and hurl an insult, but instead it was Grandad.

"What's weighing on you?" Grandad asked, joining Sam at the wooden railing.

"Nothing much," Sam answered. "Just restless, I guess."

Runt pushed his head into Grandad's hand, demanding attention. Grandad rubbed one of his ears. "I know you like having some space, but something's eating at you," Grandad said, glancing at Sam, expression indecipherable. "This doesn't have to do with that place you're buying in Wyoming, does it?"

"Who told you?"

"Does it matter?"

There were few people Sam respected as much as his grandfather. There were few people he couldn't bear to disappoint, but Melvin Wyatt's opinion mattered a lot to Sam.

Melvin was both dad and grandfather rolled up into one. Joe was the only one of them to remember their real dad, and life before they came to Montana. But Grandad had done right by them. He was strict and yet loving. There were always consequences for screwing up, but when the chips were down, no one had their backs more than Grandad.

"Does Mom know?"

"Not yet. But you should tell her before she hears it from someone else."

Sam nodded, aware he wasn't as close to his mom as some of his brothers and he wasn't sure why. Growing up, he just hadn't needed her attention as much as the others, and maybe it was because there had been a lot of babies in quick succession that he'd just grown up a bit faster, but Sam had learned early, if he needed something done, go to Grandad. If he had a question, talk to Joe. He'd just understood early in life that his mom had enough worries without him adding to them. "You upset about it?"

"You can't spend your life in Joe's shadow," Melvin answered, "but I do think Joe will take it hard when he learns you're moving that far away. This is a big place for one person to run by himself."

"He has you."

"I'm not going to live forever, son."

Sam's chest tightened. "Don't say that," he said gruffly, turning to give his grandfather a fierce hug. "We all need you."

His grandfather hugged him back, giving him a firm pat on the back, before letting him go. "So it's not just the ranch that's troubling you. This is about your girl, too, Ivy."

Grandad said it like a statement, not a question, and Sam was always amazed by his grandfather's perceptiveness. There was little Melvin Wyatt missed. "She hasn't been my girl for a long time, Grandad."

"You still care about her."

"I promised her mom I'd keep an eye on her, and I haven't done a good job doing that. Something's wrong but Ivy's not telling me."

"What do you think is wrong?"

"That's the problem. I can't figure it out. She must be in some kind of financial trouble because she's living in squalid little house behind Marietta's railroad tracks. She's sold Belle—"

"Her mare?"

Sam nodded. "It doesn't make sense. Ivy is good with money. Careful. When we used to travel, Ivy did all the finances and kept us on a budget." Sam looked at his grandfather. "Even her personality is different. She's closed. Hard. I don't understand."

"And you've asked her?"

"She won't talk about it."

Melvin said nothing for a minute. "What do you want to do?"

"Make her talk. Get her to open up. See if there isn't some way I can help."

"Then listen to your gut."

Sam nodded. "I'm going to see her. Right now."

IVY'S FEET HURT, and her head thumped with a headache she

hadn't been able to kick all day, despite regular dosing of headache medicine. Now at twelve forty-five a.m., she was more than ready to go home, but still had fifteen minutes until closing. Thank goodness it wasn't the weekend because then she'd be here until two.

It had been a slow night and Ivy had told Lucy to go on home, as Pia had left an hour earlier. Normally, Aaron, the bouncer, would be here but he had a bout of the stomach flu and Ivy didn't want him around. The stomach flu wasn't on her list of favorite things.

There were only two men in the bar, and they were familiar faces, customers who came in once or twice a week, but once they started drinking, only left when kicked out. They were nice about getting kicked out, though, and never caused trouble. They also made her feel safe because, even inebriated, they wouldn't let anything happen to her.

She was caught off guard then, when the door opened and Sam walked in, shoulders of his black leather coat dusted with snow. He took off his black hat, gave that a shake, and her heart did a painful little leap. He was ruggedly handsome, his high cheekbones and strong jaw appealing as ever. She'd had a weakness for his face from the moment she first met him, years ago, and she hated that her heart still sped up every time she saw him. Even in Calgary last summer, he'd made her feel slightly breathless, and incredibly restless, and she realized then that she'd never not respond to him. The attraction was physical—elemental—and, coupled with their history, she still felt such a strong connection to him.

Sam's gaze met hers briefly, before sweeping the nearly empty bar, and returning his attention to her. There was something in his blue gaze tonight that sent a tingly shiver down her spine because she knew he was there for her. She could see it in his eyes, and the set of his firm lips. Sam wasn't one to keep late hours, and he didn't like to drink, so him showing up at closing meant he either had news for her, or he was checking up on her. Either way, adrenaline danced through her, making her hands tremble as she reached into the hot sudsy water to finish washing the remaining glasses.

"What brings you this way?" she asked, as he pulled out a barstool and sat down in front of her.

Again his steady blue gaze met hers, expression inscrutable. "Thought I'd swing by, see if everything was good here."

As if the Wyatt Ranch was just down the street and not an half hour away. "That's a long trip for you, especially going home."

"I like driving at night."

She paused, hands buried in the hot water. "You don't need to worry about me, Sam. I'm not your responsibility."

"I know. But what kind of friend would I be if I didn't make sure you were safe?"

A lump filled her throat and she smashed the fresh wash of emotion, not wanting to feel more than she already did. Sam wasn't easy for her. Seeing him every day was proving far too bittersweet. "All good here," she answered huskily.

"Just about to close up and head home."

"I didn't see your truck in the parking lot. Where is it parked?"

"It's in the garage. Needs a new tranny."

"How are you getting to and from work?"

"I walk."

"At this hour?"

"Sam, it's just around the corner. Ten minutes at most."

"That's not okay."

"I've been doing it for weeks and nothing has ever happened."

"That doesn't mean it's safe."

"This is Marietta. Trust me, nothing's going to happen."

"Well, I'm driving you home tonight."

She wanted to protest but she'd just be wasting her breath. Once Sam made up his mind about something, nothing could change it. "Thanks."

He drummed his fingers on the counter. "Tell me about this lady you rent from."

"She's quite a character."

"What's her name?"

"Joan Marcel."

"Where's the house?"

"I thought Billy told you all of this already."

"He didn't give me specifics," Sam answered.

Ivy rinsed a set of glasses and placed them in the drying rack. "The house is at the end of Chance, near the apartment complex. It backs into that empty land bordering the highway."

"Does she treat you alright?"

"As long as I pay my rent, she leaves me alone."

Sam didn't seem to be reassured by that. "Maybe I should check the place out."

Ivy laughed as she rinsed the next glasses. "And what would you do if you didn't approve? Fix the locks on the doors? Add a safety bar to the window?"

"So it isn't safe."

"Joan offered me one of her handguns, just in case. I declined it."

Sam's expression was priceless. He looked absolutely horrified. "Your mother would not be okay with this."

"My mother would say Joan's an original, and she is. And honestly, if I didn't feel safe, I wouldn't be there. I promise you that."

Sam said nothing for a moment before blurting, "What did Wes think of your place?"

Her insides did a sickening free fall. "Let's not talk about him," she said.

"Not together anymore?"

"I thought we established this yesterday. *No.*"

"That bad?"

"Pretty much."

Silence stretched and then he broke it, saying, "I'm worried about you. The whole family is."

"No need to worry. I'm fine."

"Mom wants you to join us for Christmas dinner," he said. "In fact, she's counting on it."

Ivy's heart did another tumble. "That's awfully nice of her, but I already promised George I'd work Christmas." She saw his expression and shrugged. "Everyone else has family—"

"Mom's not going to be happy."

Ivy believed him. His mom ruled the Wyatt roost. "Tell her I'm sorry."

"She'll want you to come another time."

"That would be nice."

"In the meantime, why don't we grab breakfast or lunch?"

"Sam, you're not home often and your family wants to spend time with you."

His gaze narrowed. "That doesn't mean we can't find an hour to sit down and talk."

The last two customers pushed back from the bar and shouted goodbye before walking out.

Ivy looked at Sam. "Let me grab their glasses and we can head out, too."

"You don't have to wash them?"

"I'll just do it tomorrow."

Sam put on his coat and hat and waited while she tidied up, turned out lights, and checked the back door, sliding the dead bolt, before following her outside while she locked the front door. It was bitterly cold tonight, the wind gusting, blowing the light recent flurry of snow in billowing circles.

Sam hunched his shoulders against the biting wind. "What time do you start tomorrow?"

"I'm closing again so not until four."

"Let's have lunch before you start."

She zipped her parka all the way closed and pictured the basket full of dirty clothes in her room, and the sheets on her bed in need of washing. At the same time, a lunch out would be such a nice change. She spent far too much of her free time alone. "Could we get through a whole lunch without fighting?"

"We didn't argue tonight, did we?"

Ivy wrinkled her nose, trying to remember. "I guess not."

"So let's have lunch at Main Street Diner," he said, walking her to the passenger side of his truck and opening the door. "You love their buffalo burgers."

"I do," she agreed. "Haven't had one in years though. Do they still serve them?"

"It's a diner staple," he answered, closing the door after she'd climbed in. Once he was in the driver's seat he added, "Let's prove that we can be friends."

*Friends.*

*We can be friends.*

Sam's words stayed with Ivy for a long time after he'd dropped her off at Joan's house, staying out front watching her until she was safely in the house.

In her room, Ivy changed into pajamas before going to the bathroom to wash her face and brush her teeth.

*Friend. Friends.*

They sounded like nice words, so why did they not feel nice when she repeated them to herself?

In bed, she pulled the covers up, telling herself she should be grateful that Sam and she were talking, and friendly, after their painful breakup.

She should be glad she had a friend like Sam Wyatt—he was a great friend to have on one's side—but having been his girlfriend, having been on the most inner circle of his world, being a *friend* seemed almost like a failure. Ivy shouldn't look at it that way. Friendship wasn't something to sneer at. But her feelings for Sam were still so strong... she hadn't realized just how strong until she was near him again.

No wonder after their breakup, they put so much distance between them.

No wonder their breakup had been so final and complete.

She couldn't handle being near him, or on the fringe of his life. He was so big, so intense, so everything to her that it was all or nothing, and so he became nothing, and her heart broke further.

She never wanted to feel pain like that again. It was a loss and a grief, and different from grieving over her mother's death. It was a grief because she'd hoped, maybe even expected, that Sam would come back for her. Fight for her. Instead, he let her go and moved on, never once looking back.

It killed her that he could move on so easily. She didn't. She couldn't. She'd hurt, and hurt, and hurt.

It had taken almost a year to feel less broken. And then, just when she thought she'd survive it—him—her mother died and the pain started again, hotter, bigger, fiercer.

She'd lost Sam. Lost her mom. She had nothing left.

No wonder she'd been so ripe for Wes to pick. Pluck.

Dominate.

She hadn't even realized it was control and domination until it was too late, and he'd ensnared her in a web she was still trying to escape.

Anxious, unsettled, Ivy grabbed her phone and went to the kitchen to see if any of her chocolate milk was left. Chocolate milk was her go-to drink when she couldn't sleep, or needed something soothing. She needed something soothing tonight. Her heart felt raw and she felt sad. *"I miss you, Mom,"* she whispered as she put the milk back into the fridge.

And then, for no reason she could understand, she texted Sam. *"Hey Sam, it's Ivy. I have a new number. Just wanted you to have it in case you need to cancel tomorrow."*

He answered back immediately. *"Thanks for the #. Not canceling."*

She answered with a ☺

He answered, *"I'll pick you up at one."*

She texted, *"I have errands to do. I'll meet you there."*

*"Sounds like a plan."*

SAM CLOSED HIS phone, returning it to his pocket when he felt his brothers staring at him. "Something wrong?" he asked, glancing at the TV screen and the show was still on, so that wasn't the issue.

"You were texting," Tommy said.

"And?" Sam asked.

"You don't text," Tommy answered. "Like, you've made it clear. You. Don't. Text."

Sam didn't know if he was annoyed or amused. "It was Ivy. She wanted me to have her new phone number."

"Why did she change it?" Billy asked.

Tommy looked at Billy. "Who changes their number anymore?"

"I don't know," Sam answered, realizing his brothers had a point.

He didn't know anyone, especially in their business, who changed their cell number. It was how everyone found you. It was how you entered events. It was how—

*Wes.*

Sam's jaw clamped down, back teeth grinding hard. Had she changed her number so Wes couldn't find her?

Fresh anger, and concern, washed through him. Ivy used

to be so attached to her phone. She was always posting new photos on Instagram and Snapchat. Sharing stories about her horses, and competing, and her performance at each rodeo. He used to say she spent more time looking at her phone than she did looking out the window.

Sam glanced over at his brothers. "Do either of you use Instagram?"

"We both do," Tommy said.

"Can one of you look up Ivy? Check her profile out?"

Sam waited impatiently while Billy visited her Instagram account profile, and scrolled down to look at the photos. "They're all old," Billy said. "She hasn't posted anything since August 4."

"Not since August?" Sam said, concern growing.

"And she must have deleted her Snapchat," Tommy added. "Her profile there is gone."

"That seems weird," Billy said. "She used to use Snapchat to communicate with us, well, with everyone."

It was weird. More than weird.

New phone number, no Snapchat, and nothing in over four months on Instagram. It was as if Ivy wanted to go off the grid… disappear. The lead weight in his gut grew bigger, colder. What was going on?

IVY STOOD AT the window of the room she was renting from Joan, looking out at the sky. It was snowing hard, flurries of white, and it had been coming down since the early hours of the morning, piling up on the fence, and covering Joan's black Toyota, with the perpetual flat tire, in white.

The snow was beautiful and she felt happy. She loved fresh snow, and she was going to be having lunch out today—with Sam Wyatt no less.

Maybe that was why her heart was humming and she felt restless and eager to be out. She needed to move, walk, work some of this adrenaline through her. She shouldn't be so excited about lunch. And she most definitely shouldn't feel… giddy.

Glancing at her phone she saw she still had hours before lunch. She needed to remain productive and keep her laundry going.

Ivy headed out the kitchen door to the detached garage where the washer and dryer were.

The washing machine was still going but almost at the end of the cycle. She checked the load in the dryer, and everything there was almost done, too.

Ivy crossed her arms over her chest, keeping warm while she waited. She was lost in thought when she got a whiff of smoke. Glancing up, Ivy spotted Joan in the doorway, a cigarette between her lips.

"Am I holding you up?" Ivy asked.

Joan shook her head, and taking the cigarette from her mouth, exhaled a stream of smoke. "You had a call last night, from a fellow named Weston."

Ivy stiffened, skin prickling. "Weston?"

"That's what I thought he said when he asked for you."

An icy shiver coursed through her. Ivy suddenly felt light-headed. "Did he say anything else?"

Joan took a drag on her cigarette, before blowing out a perfect smoke ring. "Wanted to know where you were working."

"Did you tell him?"

"No. I figured you could do that. He's calling back in a couple hours. Wanted me to be sure to let you know. So now you know."

Joan returned to the house and Ivy remained in the small icy garage, chilled all the way through.

She'd known he'd find her one day.

She'd just hoped it wouldn't be this soon.

Ivy's phone buzzed and panic flooded her even as she reluctantly reached for the phone in her back pocket. She let out a shuddering breath when she saw it was Sam. Thank God.

*"It's snowing pretty hard. Sure you don't want a lift?"* he texted.

*"I'm good. Thanks, though."*

*"Great. And whoever gets there first, grab a table."*

Ivy finished her laundry, put her clean clothes away, and made up her bed with fresh sheets. She moved quickly, determined to get out of the house before Wes called. Bed made, she brushed her hair, patted her back pocket, checking for her phone, reassured by the rigid outline through the stiff denim of her Wranglers, and then grabbed her coat and purse.

Outside, she walked briskly. The snow was still falling, but less heavily. The world was still and serene, little traffic at the moment, and yet she couldn't see the beauty, not when she kept going hot and then cold, her heart racing, her stomach queasy.

If Wes had the landline phone number for Joan's house, then he knew exactly where she was, which meant, he was on his way to find her.

But Wes couldn't find her. Wes was bad news. She couldn't allow him to be in her life anymore.

Ivy arrived at Main Street Diner first, and after stomping the packed snow from her boots and brushing it from her coat, she went inside where it was warm and smelling of coffee and grilled meat and onions. The diner was still in the middle of the lunch crowd and she was taken to a small table for two in the back corner. The quiet corner suited her fine and when the waitress asked if she wanted something to drink, Ivy ordered a coffee, black, but once it arrived, she couldn't make herself drink it. Instead, she clasped the warm cup in her hands, and stared out one of the frosted windows featuring a happy snowman, trying to ease the chill around her heart.

She'd tried too hard to manage everything on her own. She'd tried hard to be tough and independent, rebuilding her life, and her finances. She hadn't opened a new checking account in Marietta. She used a PO box for bills and mail. How did Wes find her? How could he track her down to Joan's?

Ivy wanted to tell Sam everything, but he wouldn't like it. And Sam was old school. He helped little old ladies across the street and made sure lost ducklings found their mother. He wouldn't be okay with Wes's behavior. He wouldn't stand idly by if Wes threatened her in any way. And Wes would when he came to town.

She exhaled slowly, blinking away the stinging sensation in her eyes.

"You look lost, Ivy girl," Sam said, his voice low and quiet.

She glanced up at him and ran a fingertip beneath an eye, making sure it was dry. "I didn't hear you approach."

"It's pretty noisy in here today. I think the kids are out of school now for vacation." Sam peeled off his coat, hung it on a hook on the brick wall and then sat down across from her, taking up all the space in the small corner, making her wish now she'd been given a big booth.

"When are you going to trust me?" he asked, reaching out for one of her hands, and holding it between his. "We're supposed to be friends."

His hands were rough but warm, and they felt good. He was reassuringly familiar, and safe. "I trust you," she answered unsteadily.

"Then why won't you confide in me? Something's going on and it's tearing you apart."

She lifted her head and looked into his blue eyes; eyes so clear always reminded her of the Montana sky. "It's complicated."

"I know I didn't go to an Ivy League college, but I'm not an idiot. What's happened? And I know something has— new phone, different number, no social media anymore. You're working in Crawford County, pouring drinks, talking about retiring from barrel racing. Who are you running from?"

"Not running from—" She broke off, overwhelmed, emotions running high. Ivy gulped a breath and shook her head, tears starting to fill her eyes. "Just a sec. Let me just pop into the ladies' room. I'll be right back."

HE SAW THE tears in her eyes, as well as the way she bit down into her bottom lip as she rushed from the table. It was all he could do to keep his seat and not chase after her. If she needed a moment, he'd give her a moment. But this time, he wasn't going to drop the subject, and he wasn't going to accept that everything was okay.

Ivy returned five minutes later, smiling brightly, but the tip of her nose was pink and her eyes overly bright. "Did you order?" she asked, sitting back down at their table.

"You haven't even looked at the menu yet."

"I was going to do the buffalo burger, with cheese. And fries."

Sam signaled for the waitress and she headed over. He placed the order, and made small talk, thinking there was time enough to talk about serious stuff after they ate. Ivy was so high-strung, he had to keep things relaxed until she was more at ease. "My brothers say hello."

"Say hello back." She looked up at him from beneath her lashes, expression wistful. "I miss them, Tommy and Billy."

"They miss you, too."

"I wish Tommy had talked to me at the bar, and not just kept his distance."

"I think he was shocked to see you there."

She made a face. "Wolf Den's a bar, not a brothel."

"Yeah, but they remember you being a church girl."

"I still go to church, still read my Bible and pray."

His gaze swept her pretty face, lingering on her eyes before dropping to her lips. It was on the tip of his tongue to ask if her prayers were working, but that didn't seem fair, or kind, and she was in desperate need of kindness.

And so they used the twenty minutes while waiting for their food to chitchat. He told her he needed to get his mom a birthday gift but it was always hard to shop for her. Ivy asked if they had a Christmas tree yet, and he said it was the biggest one they'd ever had. They discussed who was in Las Vegas this year and then finally lunch arrived.

Sam forced himself to be patient while she ate her burger, and still held back while she slowly picked her way through her french fries. But as she began to play with her food instead of eat, he knew he had to push for information. "Ivy, are you hiding from Wes?"

Her eyes widened and her cheeks lost color. "Why… why…"

"Just a yes or no, babe."

She fidgeted with her plate and then mashed a fry. "Wes and I did not part on… good terms."

Sam studied her pale, pinched face. There was so much she wasn't saying. He felt the rise of impatience not because he needed a story, but because he was worried about her. This was not the Ivy he knew. This was an Ivy but full of hesitation and secrets. "Tell me everything, Ivy. I want the truth."

She mashed another fry into the small pool of ketchup on her plate. "Wes isn't who he appears to be. He's not someone I want to be around. In fact, he's someone I never want to see again."

"He cheated on you?"

She laughed. "If only it was that easy." She glanced up at Sam, expression shuttered. "He's not a nice man. He's not a good person."

Sam had to take a breath to stay calm. "All this time I thought you and Wes were solid. He certainly seemed devoted to you. You were always together these past couple of years."

"Wes wouldn't let me do anything without him. We were always together because we always had to be together." Her mouth opened, closed. "I don't even like telling you these things. It's humiliating."

"You can trust me, Ivy."

"Yeah, but you won't respect me when you know everything. *I* don't respect me—"

"Are you telling me he was controlling?"

She let out a soft inarticulate sound. "Wes is the most controlling person I have ever met. He was also impossible to escape from. I couldn't breathe in that relationship. I couldn't be me in that relationship. After a while, there was no me anymore, there was just him, holding the puppet strings."

"Why didn't you ask for help? I would have helped you. *Any* of us would've helped you."

Her voice cracked. "I was just in too deep. I didn't know what to do. I didn't know who to trust—"

"You didn't know who to trust? Ivy, you have so many friends on the circuit. You have so many friends who care about you—"

"It didn't feel like it." She blinked, looked away. "After Mom died, I was just so alone. I'd never felt so alone before. And then Wes arrived and he seemed to pick up the pieces."

"You were not in pieces. Your life wasn't in pieces—"

"My mom died without ever letting me know how sick she was! She let me think she had mono, something like that.

I never knew she had cancer, and if I'd known I would have been there that last year, instead of competing."

"Your mom respected you, and she was proud of your career."

"She was more important than my career."

"I think she just didn't want to be a burden."

"Then that was selfish of her, because by the time I knew what was going on, it was over. And it broke my heart that she'd died without me. And that's when Wes showed up; when my heart and life were in pieces. Wes stepped in when I couldn't think straight. I wasn't eating, or sleeping, and then he swept me right into this fairy-tale romance, and for a while it was good. Then little by little, I began to see there was a price to be paid for being Wes's girlfriend. He wanted to tell me how to dress, he wanted to shape me, he wanted to make decisions about which horse I rode and which rodeos I entered, and which sponsors I was to sign with, or let go."

"That's not something he should have been doing. Ever."

"I know, but when I was first struggling with Mom's death, I was completely numb and in a fog, and I welcomed his help. I found it useful, and helpful, to talk about sponsorships and opportunities with him. He is so connected and respected in the business that getting his feedback was good, but then over time it became more than just feedback. Wes began making the decisions for me and it was no longer my choice." She stopped talking then and just stared down at her plate.

Sam couldn't bring himself to speak, too blown away by what Ivy had told him. He'd had no idea that things were so bad for her, no idea that Wes had been such a dark, sinister influence. "We were both in Calgary in July. You should have told me then, Ivy. I would have helped you. My brothers would have helped you."

"I wanted to reach out." She bit down into her lower lip. "A half dozen times I nearly approached you, but Wes was always hovering. He wouldn't give me any breathing room and I wasn't yet prepared to lose everything—"

"Lose everything?"

"My money, my savings. He had access to everything—"

"How? I don't understand."

"As my manager, he arranged for automatic deposits instead of checks. He had payments sent to him so I could focus on competing."

"You don't like anyone touching your money."

"He said he managed a number of competitors and this was how it was done." She reached up and combed her fingers through her long hair, before tucking the heavy loose strands behind an ear. "I wanted him to stop managing my career, but I couldn't figure out an exit strategy. Wes had very publicly taken on the role of my manager, and everyone went to him. My sponsors stopped asking me what I wanted and what I needed, and when I told Wes I wasn't comfortable, he… he got ugly."

Sam growled deep in his throat and stared out the big

window overlooking Main Street. It was all he could do to stay in his seat, nearly impossible when he wanted to thrash something—someone—badly. "What do you mean by things got ugly?" he asked when he could trust himself to speak. "Did he touch you? Lay a hand on you?"

"He never slapped me. He never punched me—"

"For God's sake, Ivy, did he touch you? Did he ever put a hand on you in anger?"

"He pushed me. He shook me. Stuff like that."

Beneath the table, Sam's hands clenched into fists. He was so angry, unbelievably angry, and yet he didn't want to lose his temper. Ivy hated conflict. She didn't like yelling. "How often?"

"Would it make you feel better if it only happened one time?"

"No. And I don't think it was just one time. I'm thinking he was aggressive with you for a long time, and I'm thinking there is a lot you're still not telling me."

She didn't speak for a long time and the silence was almost worse than her words. "The bottom line," she said at length, "is that I shouldn't have trusted him. I shouldn't have let him into my life. Once I did, I was cornered, and I'm not proud of it, and I'm not comfortable admitting how bad it was, but I did get away from him, and I've been happy here… until now."

"What does that mean?"

"My landlady, Joan, just told me today that Wes phoned

the house last night, while I was at work. He told her he was going to call again today." Ivy looked at Sam. "I don't know how he figured out where I was staying. And if he has Joan's landline, he has her address. I'm sure he's on his way to Marietta now."

Sam tossed down his crumpled paper napkin. "Are you done eating? 'Cause I need to get out of here," he said curtly.

She nodded and Sam, after glancing at the bill tucked face down beneath the condiment holder, put a couple twenties on the table. "What time do you have to be at work today?" he asked.

"Four."

"We have time for a walk. Feel like stretching your legs?"

"Yes."

# CHAPTER FOUR

T HEY SET OFF toward the domed courthouse, with the massive Christmas tree in the courtyard. Oversized colored balls filled the tree, along with a shimmering red tinsel garland. Copper Mountain rose up behind the century-old courthouse, the mountain peak white, completely covered in snow. Fresh snow covered much of Crawford Park, too, but the paths had already been shoveled clear. Streetlamps lining the park's paths were decorated with greenery and more bright red bows. Crawford Park, like downtown Marietta, looked like a scene straight from a TV Christmas movie, only Sam's mood was not Hallmark friendly.

"Sam, I'm sorry—" Ivy started.

He cut her off. "I'm not mad at you."

"But you're upset."

"I'm going to destroy him," Sam said tightly, glancing down at her. "I will break every bone in his body—"

"Sam, that won't help. You can't touch him. He'll have you charged with assault so fast you won't know what hit you."

"Yeah, but I'd have the satisfaction of knowing what hit him."

She smothered a laugh. "I know you love talking with your fists, but this isn't the time. It will just make things worse for everyone."

Sam stopped walking and faced her. Her cheeks were pink from the cold air, and her dense black lashes made her light green-brown eyes brighter. And he realized all over again how much he'd missed her, and how awful it had been letting her walk away from him. It was without a doubt the hardest thing he'd ever had to do. "I'm not going to let him hurt you ever again."

"We'll need a plan," she said, shoulders hunching. "He's smart. Scary smart."

Sam rolled his eyes. "Wes is a poser. He's a phony. He pretends to be someone he's not. If he was that bright, he wouldn't have had to trap you. Bully you." Sam reached out and gently lifted a wispy tendril of dark hair from her flushed cheek. "No man should ever treat a woman that way, let alone someone like you."

And like that, the promise he'd made to Ivy's mom, Shelby, the promise that he'd look out for her, keep her safe, flashed through his mind. He hadn't kept that promise. He'd done a few things for her, mostly financial things, but it wasn't enough, not when she'd been in danger.

Sam didn't know if he reached for her, or she moved first, but suddenly Ivy was in his arms, and he was hugging her close, holding her as if he'd never let go.

It felt impossibly good to have her in his arms. She was tall and slim and despite the heavy winter coats, fit against him perfectly, her cheek just beneath his shoulder.

"I'm scared, Sam," she whispered. "Scared that you'll get in trouble and I'll be left to deal with him—"

"Not going to do that to you, Ivy," he interrupted gruffly. "I won't be stupid. I promise not to do anything that would make your situation worse." He stepped back and tipped her face up so he could see her eyes. "We'll outsmart him. Outmaneuver him. It's going to be alright."

She smiled unsteadily, expression still anxious. "I almost feel like I can breathe again."

"What scares you the most about him? That he'll hit you, hurt you, what?"

"It's just the way he talks to me. Like I'm… stupid." Her voice dropped, and her smile faded. "Like I'm… worthless."

"So, why did you stay with him?"

"I didn't even realize what was happening until I'd lost confidence in me, and my ability to make good decisions. Just falling for him was such a bad decision. I still don't understand how I couldn't see who he was. That I couldn't see how snaky and manipulative he was. That I couldn't see the truth." She swallowed hard. "And once I did understand, he'd taken over so much of my career that I was trapped."

Sam pushed another tendril away from her face, this one having tangled on her lashes. He was still raging on the inside, his pulse was thudding hard and heavy in his veins. He really wanted to destroy Wes. He was itching to do some damage. "Do you have a plan, Ivy, or should I come up with one?"

"To be honest, I don't have a plan yet. I have so many questions—like, where is my money, and what has he done with all the sponsorship money and the income from Mom's place—but then just thinking about facing him makes me want to throw up. Because here's how it will go when I do see him. He'll act nice. He'll express concern for me, and surprise that I wasn't happy. And then the moment he gets me alone, he'll flip, and begin going at me, saying that I'm stupid and worthless and nothing without him—"

"I am going to kill him. I will—"

"Sam, you can't do that. I need you." Her voice cracked and her eyes welled with tears. "Please."

"Not leaving you, and probably not going to actually kill him—"

"No wounding or badly bruising, either."

"So light bruising works?"

Ivy brushed her tears away and laughed. "I'm not going to answer that."

"So you're giving me permission to—"

"Let's get some hot chocolate," she said. "Talk about something else. This conversation is worrying."

"That's your plan?" he asked incredulously. "Change the subject? Order hot chocolate?"

"I don't know that we're going to have all the answers now. A lot will depend on when Wes arrives."

"Listen, babe, I know you hate conflict, but Wes could be here in Marietta right now for all we know."

Her crooked smile faded. "You think so?"

"I don't know and that's the point. We don't know when he'll be here, and we have to be prepared. Are you?"

She looked up into his eyes, her gaze searching. "I'm more prepared now that I told you about my situation. I feel a lot safer already. You make me feel safe."

"Because you are safe with me," he said gruffly.

"I know." She hesitated. "And I'm grateful, I am."

"You don't need to be grateful. You're important to me."

"As you are to me." She drew a slow breath. "Can I make a confession?"

"Yes."

"I think one of the reasons I took the job at the Kruse ranch was that I felt safer here in Paradise Valley than anywhere else. I knew your family was close. I knew in the back of my mind I could reach out to Joe if things got really bad." She searched his expression. "I'm sorry, but at the same time, not sorry because I'd run out of options."

"Wes is wrong. You're not stupid. You're very smart and strategic. Coming here was the right thing to do. Wes might try to dominate you when you're in his world, but this isn't his world, and he doesn't belong here." Sam reached out, hooked a finger around her belt buckle and pulled her toward him. "You, though, belong here. You're a Montana girl, through and through. Now let's celebrate smart decision-making with a hot chocolate."

"Only if it's my treat."

"Then I'm ordering a large with extra whipped cream."

As they headed back down Main Street, Ivy tucked her hand through the crook of his arm and Sam's chest tightened. Again, he thought of the promise he made Shelby, a promise he'd honored in only the most technical sort of way. "What will you do when Wes shows up?"

"Besides call you?"

He huffed a soft laugh. "Yes."

She chewed on her lip. "Will I need to do anything else? He won't bother me, not if you're around."

"You sound awfully confident about that."

"I am. Let's face it, he's not going to want to take you on, much less you and your brothers, and everyone knows you're a package deal. Fight one, fight all."

Sam smiled ruefully. She wasn't wrong. "We don't do *that* much fighting."

Ivy squeezed his arm. "Come on, Sam, you didn't get the name Slugger for playing baseball."

STANDING ON THE sidewalk in front of Copper Mountain Chocolates, with her large cup of hot chocolate topped with extra whipped cream, Ivy felt better than she had in a very long time. Her problems weren't solved. Her fear was still there. The year and a half of being in an abusive relationship had damaged her self-esteem. She'd damaged her self-esteem by remaining in such a relationship, but there was light at the end of the tunnel.

Hope.

On one hand, nothing had truly changed and yet, at the same time, everything had changed.

She wouldn't have to deal with Wes on her own anymore. She had a friend, an ally, in Sam, and there was no one better to have in your corner than Sam Wyatt.

She glanced up at him, and her heart did that funny little double beat it always did when he was near. He might not be the most extroverted Wyatt, but he was solid. Strong. Tough. Honest. Loyal. As long as she'd known him, he'd done the right thing, even when it wasn't the popular thing. She knew without a doubt, she'd be safe now, and that was such a relief she felt lighter. Almost dizzy. It was as if Christmas had come early.

"You have whipped cream right there," he said, gesturing to her upper lip.

She swiped the corner of her upper lip with her tongue.

"You missed it," he said.

"Maybe you should help me," she said, lifting her face.

His blue gaze met hers and then dropped to her mouth. "Maybe I should," he answered, before his head dropped and he covered her mouth with his.

His lips were cool, and yet warm, and he kissed her with just enough pressure to make every nerve ending in her body come to life. "Wow," she whispered when he finally lifted his head. "I think you got it."

His eyes glowed down at her, eyes warm. "I don't think you can order any more hot chocolate. Makes you taste too sweet."

"You'll just have to have self-control, Sam, because I fully intend on having hot chocolate every day now."

His mouth quirked. "I forgot how much you like trouble."

She started to smile but then the smile faded as she thought of Wes. No, she didn't like trouble. Real trouble wasn't fun. "I think we do need a plan," she said quietly. "I don't think I'm prepared for Wes. Whenever I think of him, I just get sick and scared."

"I've been thinking about this, too, and I want to move you up to the ranch. It's the best place for you. From what you've said, your landlady isn't going to protect you, and you walking to and from work is just asking for trouble. But Wes won't come up to the ranch. He won't come anywhere near the ranch." Sam glanced at his watch. "We still have an hour and fifteen minutes before you start work. That's plenty of time to get you packed up and out of Joan's house. I think we should do it right now."

"And then what?"

"We'll pack you now, I'll drop you off at the bar, drive

your things to the ranch, and be back to pick you up after work."

"That's a lot of driving back and forth, Sam. I don't want to make you my chauffeur. Why don't we wait until my truck is ready—"

"Even if your truck was ready, I'd still drive you. I'm not going to give Wes any opportunities to corner you, or get you alone. I don't trust him, and I know you don't trust him, and you're safer if we keep close tabs on you."

"*We?*" she asked.

"Joe, me, Billy, Tommy. And don't act surprised. You know how my brothers feel about you. Besides, this is Paradise Valley, Montana. Our state, our home. Wes isn't welcome here."

"You're sure your mom would be okay with this?"

"Yes. More than fine when I mentioned it to her."

"You already talked to her about it?"

"Of course. It is her house."

"And your grandad?"

"If he had his way, you'd already be there now."

Ivy smiled faintly. She had a big soft spot for Melvin Wyatt, one of the best men she'd ever known. He wasn't overly friendly, or overly talkative, but he was the essence of integrity. His word was his word, and if he said he'd do something, he absolutely followed through. "I could protest about there not being enough space for me," she said, "but honestly, it'd be a relief to know Wes isn't going to break through my window at night, or bribe Joan into letting him wait for me in my bedroom."

"You think he'd do those things?"

"I think he's upset that I got away. He was sure he had me in line." Ivy shuddered, because just thinking about the past, and Wes, made her nauseous. "Let's do it. Let's move me out of Joan's. It shouldn't take me a long time to pack. Especially not if you're willing to help load up the truck."

It was a short drive to the house on Chance Avenue, and inside the house, Ivy swiftly began emptying her drawers and taking everything from the closet and dumping them into the large suitcase she'd slid under the bed before pulling her hatboxes from the top shelf of the closet, and putting her boots and shoes into a duffel bag.

Joan stood in the doorway of the bedroom watching, making commentary between sips of whiskey. "Don't think I'm going to refund any of the rent you've paid," she said.

"I'm not asking you for anything."

"And you owe me for January since you haven't given me a thirty-day notice."

Ivy paused, looked up from the duffel bag. "I'm giving my thirty-day notice."

"And the money?"

"You'll get it."

"Now?"

"No, January 1st, when I'd normally pay you."

"How do I know you'll come back and pay?"

Ivy sighed, exasperated. "You know where I work, Joan. It's walking distance from here. If you don't get your money, you can track me down there."

Sam returned from his last trip to the truck and while he didn't push Joan from the doorway, he definitely got close, and Joan finally, reluctantly stepped back.

"Is that everything?" he asked Ivy, nodding at the duffel.

"Need to strip the bed and then I'll check the bathroom," she said, zipping the duffel.

"I'll do the bed," he answered. "You do the bathroom."

Joan wandered away then, and it wasn't long before the truck was fully packed, and Ivy's small bedroom empty.

In the truck Sam looked at Ivy. "Work now?"

She nodded.

"I'll be back for you tonight," he said, shifting into drive. "And if anything comes up, call me."

She nodded, knowing exactly what he meant by, *if anything comes up*. Anything in this case being Wes.

Later at work, during a moment of down time, Ivy shared with Pia that there was someone from her past trying to find her, and he wasn't someone Ivy wanted in her life. "His name is Wes," Ivy said. "He's a good-looking guy, and he will come across as very polite, but he's not someone I'm comfortable having around."

"I've dated someone like that," Pia said somberly. "He became a menace when I tried to break up."

"Yep. Same situation," Ivy answered. "Just wanted you to

be aware."

"I'll definitely keep an eye out," Pia said. "We Wolf Den girls got to stick together."

The rest of the day was uneventful, and Sam was back at midnight to pick her up. The bar had just a few people in it when he arrived and she still had an hour before closing.

"You're early," she said as he took a barstool at the counter.

He eased his heavy coat off. "Everyone at the house has gone to bed. Figured I might as well wait here."

Her lips twitched, knowing he was someone who liked to go to bed early. "Hard to stay awake this late?"

"I took a nap earlier. I'm good."

"So where am I sleeping tonight?"

"Joe's room."

"Where is Joe sleeping?"

"He and Sophie built their own place this year. It's a custom log cabin just down the road from the house."

"I met her, you know. Sophie came by the bar a few days ago and introduced herself."

Sam looked surprised. "I didn't know that."

"She thought I could use a friend. Suggested we get lunch and gave me her phone number, just in case."

"Sophie's great. I wasn't sure what I'd think of her because of how they met, but she's good for Joe, and makes him really happy."

"How did they meet?"

Sam's brow creased and he looked uncomfortable for a moment. "Through an ad."

"An ad? What kind of ad?"

"Joe placed one looking for a wife."

For a second, she didn't know how to respond and then she spluttered on an incredulous laugh. "You're kidding me. Why? Joe's good-looking and smart and kind. Why would he need to place an ad like that, much less for a wife?"

Sam shrugged. "He was done with romance and dating. He didn't believe in love, or want to fall in love. It was a practical thing for him. So he did what he thought was the most expedient way of finding a partner who could help on the ranch and take care of the domestic side of things."

"Sophie answered that ad?" Ivy couldn't believe it. Sophie was gorgeous and warm and funny and not at all the kind of woman who needed to answer an ad.

"Yeah, but the practical part seemed to disappear and they both fell head over heels in love. Joe is crazy about her, and she spoils him rotten. They're ridiculously happy, and that makes all of us happy."

"Your mom likes her, too?"

"Mom wasn't a fan, not in the beginning, but Sophie won her over as well."

"Your mom is a tough nut to crack."

"Yeah, but she always liked you. She was a lot harder on Sophie."

"How is your mom?"

"Moving a lot more slowly than she used to. She's in a lot of pain, and you'll see that at home she uses a walker or a cane. But if we leave the ranch, we take a wheelchair with us, just to make it easier on her. She hates the wheelchair, though, and the only time she'll agree to use it is when we go to brunch at the Graff."

"Wait. What? Brunch?"

His cheekbones turned ruddy. "It's a Sophie thing."

"You go to brunch?"

"Only when home. But Grandad, Mom, Sophie, and Joe go once a month. They pile into the truck and head to the Graff. Makes me laugh, because we're not the champagne brunch kind of family, but I do think it's good for Mom to have her outings. Sophie's been good for her. They'll bake together—well, Sophie does the work and Mom directs—and it's the same thing when it's time to organize a big family meal."

"When you have such a great family, why would you want to live so far away from them?"

He shifted on the stool, broad shoulders squaring. "It's not as if they won't be my family once I have my own place."

"But your mom and grandfather won't be around forever. Why move away now?"

"Joe has inherited the Wyatt Ranch—"

"I bet he'd be more than happy to share it with you. In fact, I bet he's thinking he alrcady shares it with you and Billy and Tommy. Have you ever discussed this with him?"

"Sophie and Joe need their own life just as much as I need mine. If they want to include Billy and Tommy, great, but I want my own place. I want to create my own history and my own traditions, and that doesn't make me a bad guy."

"I've never thought of you as a bad guy—"

"Just selfish," he interrupted.

She blushed and compressed her lips, because yes, she did used to think of him that way, but maybe Sam wasn't selfish as much as independent and stubborn. But then, she was independent and stubborn, too. Maybe that was why she and Sam used to butt heads. Maybe they both had a hard time compromising.

IT WAS A quiet drive out of Marietta, heading south on the 89 toward Yellowstone. The moon was full and the landscape covered in white. Ivy was thankful there wasn't much conversation. It had been a long day and she was exhausted. She was glad Sam didn't try to force conversation, either. Sometimes silence was best.

Flattened, she tipped her head back against the seat, closed her eyes, and just gave herself over to the hum of the truck tires on the road. It felt good to be a passenger for a moment, felt good to just let go and stop fighting, worrying, stop feeling as if she had to keep it all together. Obviously, she'd failed at both, but maybe it wasn't such a bad thing to fail, because now everything was in the open—at least, everything to do with Wes. Things had gotten out of hand with him, and she'd been troubled for far too long. Boyfriends and husbands weren't supposed to be dangerous. They were supposed to be the ones that kept you safe.

"You okay?" Sam asked, voice deep, quiet.

She opened her eyes, glanced at him, noting his somber expression reflected by the lights of the dashboard. "Yes," she said, without elaborating because what could she say?

That she'd fallen in love with a snake? That she'd been so heartbroken over her mom's death, so impossibly lonely after her breakup with Sam, that she rushed into a relationship when she should have taken time to grieve? Taken time to think? Maybe that was the worst of it. She hadn't thought, and she hadn't been wise or prudent. She'd wanted comfort, and she'd blindly thrown herself into Wes's arms as if he were a life preserver.

"You know Wes doesn't scare me," Sam said after another few minutes of silence. "Nothing about him scares me."

"I know."

"I'm not worried about having difficult conversations with him, either, and happy to sit down with him and straighten things out."

"About…"

"Your sponsors. Your career. Your finances." Sam shot her another narrowed glance. "He's still getting a piece of things, isn't he?"

She shifted miserably. "He says he gets fifteen percent of everything as my manager."

"Did you ever sign a contract, or any form of an agreement?"

"No." She forced herself to add, "At least, I don't think so."

Thankfully Sam withheld any judgment. "I suspect the sponsorship agreements were for one to three years. Most sponsorships aren't for much longer than that, which means many of the agreements should be ending. From now on, you handle your own deals, okay? Or, ask Tommy his thoughts. He's a whiz with money. He's ridiculously good when he keeps his shirt on."

Ivy smiled wryly because Tommy had a face and a body and girls went crazy for him. "That's a good idea about Tommy. He's done really well for himself financially."

"What about your other investments? Your mom's place? The rent from your tenant?"

Ivy's smile faded. "Wes claims that he's invested it all."

"Where? In what?"

"I don't know."

"Do you have access to it?"

"No. At least, not that I know of."

Sam's jaw tightened and he didn't immediately speak. Ivy cringed on the inside because every single thing he must be thinking was what she was thinking.

*How does one become so stupid...*

"Ivy?"

She swallowed hard. "Yes, Sam?"

"It's just money. It's not the end of the world."

Her eyes burned hot and gritty and she chewed on the inside of her cheek. He was being far too kind. "Here's how bad it is, Sam. I don't even know how long my tenant is in the house. Early September I wrote the family and asked them to stop making auto payments through my checking account, but I don't know if they have, or haven't. I don't look at my old checking account as Wes has access to it."

"You couldn't close it?"

"I was afraid Wes could trace me if I did that. I didn't want him to know where I was, much less which part of Montana."

"Have you opened a new checking account?"

"No. I want to, but again, I was afraid Wes would find out."

Sam's voice was quiet when he spoke next. "We need to fix this, Ivy. We need to close that account, cut off his access to your funds, alert your sponsors—"

"I'll probably lose a lot."

"I doubt you will, but even if you do, it's better than remaining in relationships that aren't good for you."

She couldn't agree with him more, and she reached out and touched his arm, giving it a light squeeze. "Thank you. For everything."

It was late when they reached the ranch, high in the Absaroka mountains. The 1930s two-story log cabin was dark except for the kitchen light over the stove. Sam asked if Ivy wanted water or anything to drink before bed and she said no, just ready to climb in bed and sleep. She couldn't remember when she'd last been so tired. Talking about Wes, and how she'd allowed him to take such control over her business affairs, just made her heartsick all over again.

# CHAPTER FIVE

IVY SLEPT DEEPLY, only waking up after the sun was shining brightly. She yawned and stretched and then needed a moment to get her bearings, not understanding how there was so much sunshine in her bedroom, or why her bed was covered in a thick red, black, and tan patchwork quilt. That was when she remembered she wasn't at Joan's anymore, but rather at the Wyatts' place, tucked snuggly into bed in Joe's old room.

Glancing at her phone she saw it was almost nine o'clock. Ivy couldn't remember the last time she slept this late—maybe because it was never quiet at Joan's—and dressed quickly, heading downstairs to see if she could still get coffee and then check in with Sam to see what time he planned on driving her in to work.

Sophie was in the kitchen at the table, writing in a notebook, and stopped writing to smile at Ivy. "Good morning. Sleep well?"

"Very," Ivy answered. "I can't believe I slept this late, though."

"It's nice to be able to sleep in now and then," Sophie

answered. "I just made fresh coffee—everyone around here drinks it all day—but there is tea, too, if you're prefer that."

"Coffee is perfect, thanks."

Sophie gestured to the line of Santa mugs on the windowsill over the sink. "Grab a mug. There is some cream in the refrigerator if you need it."

"No, I like it black," Ivy answered, filling her jolly ceramic Santa, before pulling out a chair at the table. "Will it bother you if I sit here?"

"No, not at all. Just making notes for Summer's birthday dinner. She's not here right now, by the way. Grandad took her to see a friend in Gardiner."

"None of the boys would take her?"

"They all offered but Grandad said he had an errand he wanted to run so they'd headed out together. Now I'm just trying to figure out what I'm going to make for Summer's birthday dinner. The guys said she doesn't like a fuss, but we have to do something special, don't you think?"

"Definitely."

"You'll be here Tuesday, won't you?"

Ivy grimaced. "I pretty much work every night but Sunday night, but I could help with the grocery shopping or prep."

Sophie hesitated. "Do you intend to keep working at the bar, even with everything going on?"

It took Ivy a moment to understand what Sophie was saying. "You know about Wes."

"Sam filled us in a bit."

"How much is a bit?"

"Just that Wes isn't someone we want anywhere near you."

Again the *we*, and the family coming together to help her. Their support was overwhelming. After feeling so alone for so long, she was blown away by the Wyatt family's kindness.

"I made a mess of things," Ivy confessed. "I trusted Wes and I shouldn't have."

"Love makes us do stupid things," Sophie sympathized.

A lump filled Ivy's throat. "I didn't even love him, not the way I loved Sam."

"But you had to have loved him in the beginning to start a relationship."

"Wes was an infatuation. He seemed very charming, and after dating Sam, like a breath of fresh air. You see, Sam isn't very communicative. He doesn't give a lot of compliments, or say a lot of sweet things." She looked over at Sophie. "That's not a criticism of Sam, just a fact."

"Oh, I get it. Joe is the same way."

Ivy smiled gratefully. "After Sam's and my breakup, and then my mom dying, I craved company, and Wes was suddenly there, saying how special I was, and how amazing things were with me in his life, and I just fell for it."

"But you learned things from that relationship—"

"That I'm weak."

"No." Sophie reached out and patted Ivy's arm. "That you need communication, and now that you know, you ask for it. You let your man know what you want and need, and don't apologize for having needs. We all do. Speaking of your man, he's out with his brothers doing some fencing repairs on the property."

Ivy blushed. "Sam's not my man."

Sophie just smiled.

"He's not," Ivy repeated, before adding, "What repairs are needed?"

"A big tree came down a few days ago and took a whole section of the fence out. I'm sure Joe could have managed with Billy and Tommy, but they all decided to ride out together and make it a family thing."

"That's good."

"It is. Makes Joe's happy to have his brothers with him, and you're covered, too. I promised Sam I'd drive you to work if he's not back in time as I'm working this afternoon at the salon and will be heading into Marietta just before noon."

As it worked out, Ivy did ride with Sophie, and while driving together, Sophie talked about her dairy farming family back in Tulare, and how she'd been a producer broker before she moved to Montana. Ivy was dying to know more about Sophie and Joe's early days, and what it was like moving to Paradise Valley as a modern-day mail-order bride, but Ivy didn't ask, thinking she and Sophie needed to have more of a friendship before that conversation came up.

Arriving at the Wolf Den, Ivy hung up her coat, stashed her purse beneath the bar counter and washed her hands in the sink.

"You had someone come by just a few minutes ago," Lucy said, joining her at the bar. "A cowboy. Handsome. Not a Wyatt, though, and no one I've seen before. He said he hoped to find you here and asked when you were coming in."

Ivy's stomach fell. She'd warned Pia yesterday about Wes, but hadn't yet had a chance to say anything to Lucy. "Where did he go?"

"I don't know, but he asked about your schedule and I told him I wasn't sure. He said no problem, and he'd be back later." Lucy looked uncertain. "You don't seem thrilled."

Ivy had to take a steadying breath, and then another. She couldn't let anxiety cripple her. Panicking wouldn't help. "I'm not. He's uh, not a friend of mine."

"Sorry. If I'd known—"

"It's fine, honestly. You did nothing wrong."

"Has he hurt you?"

"He's a bully. And he did his best to break me."

"But he didn't," Lucy said firmly.

"I've been working on things since coming here, to Marietta, feeling better about things. But I'm not sure I'm strong enough to deal with Wes. He's just incredibly mean. But the thing is, if you saw him, he wouldn't look like a bully. He'd seemed kind of… charming."

"That's the profile of a lot of bullies." Lucy leaned across the counter. "Bullying is repeated aggressive behavior, creating an imbalance of power. Its sole purpose is to impart physical and psychological harm."

"That pretty much sums up Wes to a *T*."

"The good news is, bullies are only as powerful as we let them be. In other words, don't let Wes be all powerful. Stand up to him. Be calm. Confident. Bullies lose power when you don't cower or cry."

Ivy nodded, agreeing with everything Lucy said, and Lucy knew this stuff. She'd taken all kinds of psychology classes when earning her criminal justice degree. "I'm glad you're here," she said. "But I don't want you to get hurt."

"I'm not going to get hurt. And neither are you. Just don't go outside with him. Don't be alone with him. That wouldn't be smart."

"Agreed."

Lucy moved on and Ivy reached for her phone, texting Sam. *"Wes showed up at the bar just before I got here. He left but he's going to be back. Thought maybe you could come to town, be here when Wes returns. I hate dragging you into this, but I'd feel more confident if you were here."*

Thankfully she got a reply almost immediately. *"On my way. See you soon."*

AT THE RANCH, Sam grabbed his truck keys, hat, coat, and wallet. His mom and grandad had just returned from Gardiner, and so he kissed his mom's cheek and headed to his truck.

Normally, it took him thirty minutes to get to town, but today he made it in twenty, a record for him. His best time previously had been twenty-two minutes, and that had been at ninety miles an hour.

Entering the dim bar, his gaze swept the room, taking in a girl on stage gyrating around a pole, a couple guys at cocktail tables close to the stage, the cocktail waitress working the room, and then Ivy behind the bar. There were men at the bar, too, but everything looked quiet, calm, but Sam could tell from Ivy's expression that she wasn't comfortable. Wes had to be one of the guys with his back to him.

Ivy's gaze met his, and then shifted to the end of the counter. She gave a faint nod. So the guy with the cowboy hat at the end was Wes. Good to know.

Sam headed to the bar, gaze riveted on Ivy. She looked particularly pretty today with her long dark hair in a tidy side braid and silver and turquoise earrings dangling from her ears.

He walked around the counter and took her in his arms. "Hey, babe," he said, dropping his head to kiss her.

Her lips were warm and soft and for a moment her mouth clung to his. It felt good to have her in his arms and even better to kiss her again.

"How're you doing?" he asked, when he finally lifted his head.

Her cheeks were flushed and her hazel-green eyes glinted up at him. He wasn't sure if she was fighting a smile or fighting tears. Either way, she was glad to see him.

"I'm good, babe." She put her hand on his bicep and gave a light squeeze. "You know you shouldn't be behind the bar. You're going to get me in trouble."

"I reckon I'm used to trouble by now. You're nothing but trouble." But he kissed her again and then walked out, passing behind the customers seated on the barstools. He could feel Wes looking at him, but so far Wes had said nothing to him. Sam knew it was just a matter of time, or maybe, Wes wanted Sam to be the first to say hello.

Sam paused, turned, and retraced his steps. "Hey, is that you, Lovett?"

Wes slowly turned and looked up at Sam over his shoulder. It took him a moment to manage a smile. "Yeah, it's me. How are you, Wyatt?"

"I'm good. Glad to be home with the family for a couple of weeks. Feels great having everybody together again." Sam paused, expression friendly. "So, what brings you here to Marietta this time of the year? Seems like you're a long way from home."

"Heading to Missoula to check out some foals, so I thought I'd stop and see Ivy." Wes smiled, but the smile didn't reach his eyes.

If anything he looked flinty and hard. And jealous as anything.

"If I'd known you were coming to town, we would have had you join us for a meal. It's unfortunate that we got plans though."

Wes glanced from Sam to Ivy and back again. "You two back together?"

"Realized I was a fool, letting her go. Begged her to come back, give me a second chance." From the corner of his eye, Sam could see Ivy's expression. She was a terrible actress. So he just kept on talking. "For a time there, it was touch and go, but I think she's just about forgiven me. We're pretty solid now, right where we want to be."

"You just got back from Vegas."

"A week ago. Tried to get Ivy out to watch me, but she didn't want to miss any of the Christmas fun here in Marietta."

"Sam, what do you want today, baby?" Ivy asked, preventing Sam from elaborating much more on his story.

"I'm considering those nachos you know I love so much."

She smiled. "Nachos today? I thought you loved the hot dogs best."

"I tell you what, I am hungry. Why don't you bring me both?" Sam glanced at Wes. "Have you tried the nachos? Dang good. Especially if you ask for some chicken on them. And then I like a little extra hot sauce—"

"Not hungry," Wes said. "But thanks for the suggestion."

"Anytime, partner."

Wes's jaw tightened and Sam could tell he was getting to Wes, especially when a few minutes later Wes pushed back his wooden barstool and followed Ivy to the far end of the bar.

IVY COULD FEEL Wes behind her even before she saw him. She stiffened and turned. "Leaving?" she said.

"I want five minutes," Wes said. "Give me five minutes. Let's go outside and talk. I haven't seen you in months and you won't even give me the time of day."

"I'm not going outside. If you want to talk, we can talk here."

"What about later, when you're off work?"

"Sam will be here. Can he join our conversation?"

"Why are you being like that? Do you have any idea how much I did for you? How much money I made you—"

"Where is it, Wes? My checking account is empty. There's maybe a couple hundred bucks in there."

"I've invested it."

"Where? In what?"

"You wouldn't understand. Stocks are complicated. They'd go right over your head. That's why I was good for you. I made you money. I made you successful—"

"I was successful without you, Wes, and I'll be successful again. Now I've got to get back to work. Goodbye."

Wes gave her a long, cold look before he stalked out of the bar. Ivy watched him go, heart in her mouth. That wasn't the best goodbye.

"What's the heavy sigh for?" Sam asked, joining her at the end of the bar.

She listened to Lucy's drink order and got busy pouring beers. "He just rattles me," she said, hands shaking as she turned on the tap.

"You did good. You didn't look rattled."

She made a face. "Well, you didn't help. I couldn't believe that hick accent you used. You couldn't have been more redneck if you tried."

"What are you talking about?"

"The whole 'I reckon,' and calling him 'partner.' I've never heard you talk like that before."

"Was just laying on the charm."

"A little bit thick, don't you think?"

"He left."

She glanced at Sam after setting two beers on the counter. "Yeah, but he's not going to disappear, not permanently. He's too upset. He's mad at me."

"What does he want from you?"

"I don't know. Power, maybe? He liked having me under his thumb. He liked making me feel small. But I'm done feeling that way."

"Good. So what's worrying you?"

"How are we going to keep up our act that we're together? He's going to come around and ask questions and poke his nose into things."

"Let him ask."

"But we won't be together always."

"No, I know that. I'm under no illusion that we're back together. We don't have a romantic relationship, and we're not committed to anything other than getting Wes off your back and out of your life."

Those were the words she wanted him to say, and yet they made her feel awful when they were said. She added another pair of beers to the counter and wiped her hands on a towel as Pia returned with her tray, loading it with the four beers. "And yet you kissed me yesterday," she said, facing Sam.

"Yes, I did."

She looked at him, waiting for more, but he said nothing else, and she felt close to losing her temper, because the kiss had been lovely, and she'd felt lovely close to him. "You can't just kiss me anytime you feel like it."

"You asked me to get the whip cream on your lip, and I did."

"There are different ways to do that. Hand, Kleenex—"

"You didn't used to be so critical of my problem-solving skills."

Exasperation warred with amusement. This was the Sam

she'd fallen in love with. This was the Sam she'd wanted to spend her life with. "I'm not being critical. You did a good job."

He smiled, creases fanning from his eyes. "Thank you."

Warm, flustered, Ivy moved down the bar, checking on her customers, refilling drinks as needed, doing her best to ignore Sam who had unleashed a whole bushel of butterflies in her middle.

She was still so attracted to him.

She still felt all the old feelings for him.

Two years apart hadn't killed her love or desire. He made her feel so much—her body hummed when he was near, skin sensitive, pulse racing. They'd been good together physically, amazing physically, but out of bed, they'd struggled to communicate, and that had become a huge problem.

Eventually, she made her way back down the counter to where Sam sat. He was staring up at the TV watching The Weather Channel. Ivy knew why it was always on—truckers liked the updates—but she avoided it. Far too much news about cold, wind, hail, and snow.

She glanced up at the TV and saw a prediction for snow and shook her head. Never good news.

"What's wrong?" Sam asked, seeing her face.

"You're leaving on the twenty-sixth for Cody. I can't stay with your family after you're gone."

"Why not?"

"It'd be weird."

"Tommy and Billy would love the company."

"They're not going to want to drive me to work every day, and babysit me at the bar—"

"Then come with me to Cody. I'll babysit you."

His words made her heart feel funny. Once that would have been a given. Where he went, she went. "That doesn't make sense. I have to work. I need my truck back. I want to get Scotch back."

"Speaking of Scotch, I do have some good news. Billy and Tommy went to pick him up for you. He'll be at our ranch soon."

Her jaw dropped. "Really?"

He nodded. "I just had a message from Billy that Scotch is in the trailer now. They're driving back to our place."

Relief washed through her. Relief and gratitude. She came around the side of the bar and flung her arms around him for a swift hug. "Thank you. That's huge. I've missed my boy so much."

Sam's arm came around her waist and hugged her back "Have you missed Scotch, too?" he asked.

Ivy laughed and taking a step back lightly kissed his cheek. His skin was so warm and he smelled of her favorite aftershave. "Yes, I've missed you a little bit, too."

"But Scotch more?"

She knew he was teasing and she was glad that things were easier between them. Lighter. "A cowgirl's got to love her horses."

"So when do we get Belle?" he asked.

Her smiled faded. "I wish."

"Why don't we buy her back?"

"Because I don't have the money—"

"I do."

"I'm not going to accept your money." Her insides felt weird, her pulse racing. "And even if I had the money, I don't know that Ian would sell her back to me."

"You won't know until you try."

"You're so sure of yourself."

"And you used to be."

She wasn't sure if it was a criticism or a comment. Either way, it was pointed and his words struck home. "I lost myself there for a bit, but I'm trying to find my way back. I know what I want now. I know what I need to do. I'm focused on saving money, and growing my business. I'm not going to depend on others anymore."

"This isn't new. You've always been that way."

"Wes—"

"Wes was a one-off. Everyone's allowed to make a mistake. Wes was yours."

"You're very kind, because Wes wasn't my only mistake." She swallowed hard. "The way I broke up with you was a mistake."

Sam said nothing and Ivy mustered her courage to continue. "I said things I shouldn't have said. I was upset, and angry, and I'm sorry, Sam."

He was silent for another moment and then his big shoulders shifted. "It wasn't a good breakup, no, but I don't suppose breakups are pretty."

"I thought you'd—" Ivy bit the recrimination back.

It didn't matter what she'd thought, or hoped. It was two years ago. So much had happened since then.

But Sam wasn't ready to move on. "You thought I'd what?"

*Come for me.* Ivy looked at him, heart in her throat. She'd wanted him to want her so much that he'd fight for her.

He hadn't.

Her phone in her back pocket vibrated and she pulled it out, checked the number. It was Jill Snyder, the Montana Circuit Director for the Women's Professional Rodeo Association. It was Jill who'd alerted Ivy to Ashley's situation, and Jill who'd asked Ivy to speak with Hope Caldwell, a young competitor near Livingston who'd broken her arm in a riding accident and had lost her confidence. "Hey, Jill, everything okay?" she asked, answering the call.

"I need to call more often if my number makes you think of doom and gloom."

Ivy heard the smile in Jill's voice. "Not doom and gloom," Ivy corrected. "But maybe trauma and tears."

"You've been a great mentor to our local girls. It's hugely appreciated."

"Happy to help. Makes me feel close to Mom."

"She taught you well."

"Yes, she did." Ivy paused. "How are you?"

"I'm good. Looking forward to Christmas and a little vacation. But first, I have a favor to ask."

"What can I do?"

"Would you have time to go see Ashley this weekend? She's been asking to see you."

"The family has already thanked me enough."

"No, it's not about that. Ashley wants to discuss something with you. But I need to warn you, her family isn't happy."

"About her talking to me?"

"About what she wants to discuss."

Ivy was beginning to understand. "She wants to ride again."

"She wants to compete again," Jill said.

Oh. Wow. Ivy bit her lip and glanced over at Sam who pretended to be minding his own business but was, she suspected, listening to every word. "And Ashley's family?" Ivy asked quietly. "Obviously they're not in favor."

"No."

"Then how am I supposed to weigh in on this?"

"What would you have done if you were just fourteen and told you'd never ride again?"

"I'd find a way to ride," Ivy said.

"Exactly."

Ivy didn't speak right away, picturing the pale, still girl

she'd last seen in the hospital in Bozeman. Then she pictured Ashley's parents. They'd been devastated, and yet fighting hard to look optimistic for their daughter's sake. "I don't want to come between her and her parents, Jill. They've all been through so much these past five months."

"Agreed. Everyone I've discussed this with feels that way. But apparently what's gotten Ashley through all the surgeries and physical therapy is the dream to return to riding, and eventually, barrel racing. I guess that's what she wants to know—can it be done?"

"And that's why she wants to talk to me."

"Yes."

Ivy drew a breath and then exhaled slowly. "I'll call her mom and get something set up for this weekend."

"That's wonderful. Let me know how it goes."

"Yep." Ivy hung up and turned around to face Sam. He was looking at her, clearly interested in the call. "You heard that?" she asked him.

He nodded.

Ivy slid the phone into her back pocket. "Do you know about Ashley?"

"She's the little girl from Belgrade who was hurt in a freak farm accident."

"She was a junior barrel racer and very promising." Ivy hesitated. "Horses have been Ashley's passion since she was a little girl, and her family really supported her."

"But the girl still wants to ride, and the parents don't

want her to."

"Ashley still wants to compete… or wants to know if it's possible."

"But she's paralyzed."

Ivy nodded once. "I see her side, I do, but I also see her parents' side. They've been through hell and back, and they're still struggling emotionally, never mind financially and I can't imagine they want to see their daughter in a saddle right away."

"And you're going to tell Ashley this?"

Ivy glanced off toward the *Ho Ho Ho* sign over the far door and remembered how she'd been at fourteen— determined, competitive, and passionately in love with a gorgeous chestnut colt named Belle.

Belle.

Ivy's heart ached for a moment and then she looked at Sam. "No. I'm going to tell her that with hard work, she can do anything she sets her mind to."

"Including competing?"

"Surely Ashley can't be the first paralyzed barrel racer to want to return to the saddle. I just need to find out who has done it, and what it took to get there."

Sam left the bar at dinnertime to head to another bar, Grey's Saloon on Main Street, where he was meeting Tommy and Billy for dinner and a beer. His brothers had offered to come to the Wolf Den, but Sam was curious to see if Wes was still in town, and if so, lurking somewhere else.

He and his brothers split up, each visiting a different restaurant between Church Street and Front Street, before meeting back up at Grey's. They grabbed one of the few empty tables between the pool table and bar. No one had seen Wes, but that didn't mean Wes hadn't checked into the Graff or one of the local bed-and-breakfasts. Wherever he was, Wes remained a threat.

LATE THAT NIGHT as Sam drove Ivy back to the Wyatt Ranch, he asked her how she'd gotten involved with Ashley.

"I was working at the Kruse Ranch, when I heard that a local girl had been paralyzed in a farm accident, and then I read that the girl was Ashley Howe, a youngster I'd worked with briefly years ago when she'd first started barrel racing. Her parents had brought her to Custer to work with Mom, and I worked with her horse and we did some lessons together.

Ivy sighed, shook her head. "Mom thought Ashley had potential to be really good. She didn't say that often, either, but she said Ashley had what it took, and she suspected she'd go far, if she stuck with the sport. So I reached out to Jill, the director for the WPRA's Montana Circuit, and told her I wanted to help the family. I already knew about the Go Fund Me, but I wanted to do more than just give money, but the main thing they needed then, was money, if Ashley was to go to the best rehab facility possible."

Sam glanced at her. "You sold Belle for Ashley's treatment?"

"I just remember what Mom had said. Ashley could be one of the great ones, and I couldn't not help. I ended up going to the hospital a half dozen times to visit Ashley until she left for her physical therapy."

"Have you seen her since?"

"No, but I want to." Ivy hesitated. "I've worked with a couple other girls in the area, though. Jill called me late September when another local girl, Hope Caldwell, had a riding accident and was suddenly scared to ride, and so I went to see her and worked with her, trying to help build her confidence back. I discovered I really liked working with the younger girls. It made me feel like I was doing something positive for the first time in a long time."

"Like mother, like daughter. Your mom did the same thing."

"Mom always said it's good to give back, and she's right. I love sharing what Mom taught me. I really enjoy teaching." Ivy gazed out her window at the dark landscape. "That's why I want to get some land and have some space. There's no reason I have to compete all the time. I can do other things. I can train horses, I can train young riders, and I can work with these junior barrel racers, giving them encouragement."

Sam reached over and placed his hand near her knee, giving it a gentle squeeze. "Shelby would be proud."

"I hope so." And then she reached for Sam's hand, holding it tight. "I miss her."

"I know you do."

They spent the rest of the drive in silence, but it was a good silence, a comforting silence where Ivy felt understood. She felt even more understood when reaching the ranch Sam asked if she wanted to go see Scotch before heading into the house.

"You know me so well," she said.

"I know who you love," he answered, even as dogs came running toward the truck, barking excitedly. Sam rolled down the window, shushing them. They immediately fell silent. "You remember the dogs? Duke, Penny, and Runt?"

"With Runt being the biggest dog I've ever seen?"

Sam grinned, parked. "Who knew he just needed some TLC?"

The dogs charged Ivy as she got out of the truck. She gave them a low firm command and they all sat down.

Sam came around the side of the truck to join her. "They've always listened to you."

"They're good dogs." She glanced at Sam as they walked to the stable. "How did it go getting Scotch back? No problems?"

"No problem at all. Kruse knew you'd be glad to have Scotch with you."

The dogs entered the stable with them, tails wagging. They knew they had to behave around the horses. Ivy spotted Scotch even as he gave her an impatient neigh.

"Hey, you," she said, going to his stall and rubbing his nose. "Long time no see," she added, giving him another rub, even as she checked out his stall, pleased to see he had hay and feed, along with a water bucket.

"Billy made sure to bring some of the feed from Kruse's here so we can introduce Scotch to the new feed gradually," Sam said. "Scotch's tack is in our tack room for now. Figured you'd want it there."

"That's great."

"Let me give you a quick tour around, as a few things changed since the last time you were here."

Sam walked her through the big barn, around the enclosed ring, pointing out feed room, tack room, and a caddy box with brushes and combs. "I have a feeling I know what you'll be doing in the morning."

"I'm almost tempted to sleep in here."

Sam grinned. "And you probably would if I said you couldn't, so I won't do that. But I could make you some tea or instant hot chocolate and send you up to your comfortable bed with something warm to drink."

"I do like my hot cocoa."

"I know you do." He slung his arm around her neck. "Let's make that hot cocoa and call it a night."

In the kitchen, while the milk warmed on the stove, Ivy leaned against the counter, and read through her emails on her phone, before sending one to Ashley's parents letting them know she was available to visit Saturday or Sunday. She didn't have to be to work until five Saturday, and she was off Sunday but wasn't sure of the Wyatts' plans as she was staying with them for now.

Sam found two mugs—a Santa mug for her and a simple brown mug for him—and got out the hot chocolate mix, spoons, and a half-empty bag of marshmallows.

When the milk began simmering, Ivy put her phone away and focused on the milk so it wouldn't burn. She waited until it turned to a slow boil and then pulled it off the burner. As she measured out the cocoa powder she glanced up and found Sam watching her intently, so intently she flushed.

"Am I doing something wrong?" she asked, suddenly shy.

"No." His voice sounded unusually deep in the quiet kitchen. "Just like seeing you here. Brings back a lot of memories."

"We had a lot of good times together," she said carefully, as she stirred first one cup and then the other, dissolving the powder into the steaming milk. "I'm glad we can be... friends. For awhile there, I thought I had lost you."

"Just had to keep my distance," he said.

A thick lump filled her throat making it hard to swallow. She looked up at him, emotions all over the place. "Did you?"

"It's what you wanted."

But it wasn't what she'd wanted. She'd wanted him. Only she'd wanted him to be more open, more affectionate, more… everything… she supposed. "Thank you for being in my corner now."

"I've always been in your corner."

She blinked, keeping the emotion in check. "One marshmallow or two?"

"Two. It's a special night."

"Is it?" she asked, handing him his cup.

"Yes. We're celebrating Scotch, and you, and all the wonderful things that will be happening in the new year."

"You think wonderful things will happen?"

"You said you wanted to get your own place."

"Yes, but that's going to take some time. I'm not in a good place financially, but I'm getting better."

"You have debt?"

"Yes."

"A lot?"

"More than I ever wanted."

"How? Where?"

The Santa mug was hot and she lifted it by the handle. "To all the credit card companies, I guess."

"You were never a big spender."

"I know. But there are my truck repairs and vet bills for Scotch, plus other stuff."

"What other stuff?"

She struggled to find the words. "Wes put a lot on my credit cards. I didn't know it at first. But he filled up the cards so I couldn't."

"Why would he do that?"

"I think it was yet another way he forced me to be dependent on him."

*"Ivy."*

He sounded so disappointed that it made her chest squeeze. "Don't be mad." She set her mug down and went to him, standing close enough that she could hook her fingers over his belt. "I messed up and I was too ashamed—"

"No more of that," he interrupted, wrapping an arm around her and bringing her up against him, thigh to thigh, chest to breast. She could feel his warmth and smell that scent that was only Sam. His hand stroked the length of her back, comforting her, and yet she felt more than comfort, she felt hunger. "Sam?" she whispered, tipping her head back.

She knew an instant before their lips met that he intended to kiss her and she was glad. Ever since yesterday, she'd craved another kiss, a real kiss this time, like the ones he used to give her, the ones that said she was his and only his.

His mouth slowly, very slowly covered hers, his lips cool but firm. He drew her even closer against him, the hard plane of his chest pressing against her breasts, his thigh shifting between her knees. She felt sensation everywhere, from the roughness of his jaw, to the tingling in her lips, to the clasp of his hands low on her hips. She'd forgotten how big he was, how muscular, and as his lips traveled across hers, drawing a hungry response, she felt almost desperate.

She sighed with pleasure as the kiss deepened, welcoming the heat and flick of his tongue against her lips, and then stroking the inside of her bottom lip.

Nerve endings danced, and she shuddered with pleasure as he cupped her butt, holding her firmly against the ridge in his Wranglers.

There had been so much passion between them, so much love. She wanted that passion back. She wanted everything she'd lost. Ivy gave herself up to the kiss, heat coiling in her middle, heat and urgency and a physical craving that left her breathless. Her hands slid up from his belt to his chest, savoring the feel of him. Hers, she thought, giving herself over to him, her man. Her heart. Always.

Suddenly the tap of a cane could be heard and the overhead kitchen light snapped on.

Sam and Ivy stepped apart but not before Summer Wyatt stood in the doorway, not looking happy at all. "We don't do this here," she said. "You know the rules."

Sam sighed. "I'm not a teenager, Mom, and it was just a kiss."

"One kiss leads to another, and I'm not comfortable with any of my sons having sex under my roof—"

"*Mom.*"

"Not until you're married. Once you're married, it's a different story." Summer looked over to Ivy. "Sex leads to babies, and I don't think either of you are ready for that. Good night."

She slowly used her cane to walk out of the kitchen for the stairs.

Ivy reached for her cocoa, now not so hot, and took a gulp. That was horrible. She felt all of fifteen again.

"Where was she?" Ivy said, as an upstairs bedroom door closed. "I didn't hear her approach."

"She must have been in the family room, waiting up. She and Grandad have a tendency to do that."

"You guys are adults."

"Yeah, but she's pretty old-fashioned when it comes to sex and marriage."

"But we did—"

"She doesn't know that," Sam answered, voice pitched low.

Ivy rolled her eyes even as she sipped her cocoa. "Oh, come on! She doesn't think her very sexy, very alpha sons have sex?"

"For her, the worst thing that could happen is for one of us to get a girl pregnant without being married."

"Doesn't she want to be a grandmother?"

"Not that way."

IVY DID NOT sleep well, despite Joe's very comfortable bed. She dreamed about Sam, and kissing Sam, and in the dream she was his girlfriend again and she was so happy. And when she woke from that dream and discovered it was almost five in the morning, and just a dream, Ivy felt as if a lead weight had dropped on her chest.

The dream had been so good… she'd hoped it was real.

She turned over, burying her face in her pillow and wrestled with all the emotions rushing through her.

She wanted her old life back, the one that included Sam and her mother. She wanted just one more Christmas with Mom. She wanted just one more chance to tell her how much she loved her. She wanted just one day of being happy, and realizing how lucky she was, and how much she had to be grateful for. A great boyfriend. An amazing mom. A wonderful life.

But she wasn't going to get her mom back, and she wasn't going to have her old life back. The only thing she could do was keep moving forward and do her best to learn from her mistakes.

Ivy left bed, dressed, and downstairs in the kitchen, discovered there was already a pot of coffee made, even though it wasn't even five fifteen. She had a feeling Grandad was up, and so she poured herself some coffee in an old mug and quietly left the house, to walk across the crunchy snow toward the barn, her breath clouding in the air. The moon was still up, and the temperature was freezing, but she had her gloves on and a cup of coffee and soon she'd be in the stable and all would be well.

The dogs came flying from the barn, enthusiastically greeting her. She snapped her fingers sharply, uttering a quiet *No*. They stopped barking and padded along beside her as she crossed the rest of the yard. Opening the stable door, Ivy felt the immediate temperature change. The stables were heated to keep the horses comfortable. Scotch wasn't very awake when Ivy reached his stall. He gave her a look that seemed almost indignant, and sipping her coffee, she gave him a pat. "Don't be so grouchy," she said, turning away to explore the barn.

There were twelve stalls, and eight were filled. Ivy peeked into the tack room again, wanting to become more familiar with how everything was stored, and then the feed room, the hay room, and finally she pushed open the big sliding door to the arena. The arena wasn't as warm as the stables, but it wasn't as frigid as outside, either. Scotch would enjoy getting a workout in here.

She returned to Scotch's stall and fed him and refilled his water bucket. He nudged her with his nose while she cleaned his stall, replacing his bedding and removing his blanket as he'd get a clean blanket tonight.

The barn and stables had been built years ago, constructed by Melvin, not for his grandsons but his two sons, JC and Samuel, as they'd competed together in rodeos since teenagers, and both went pro the same year. Melvin's sons didn't just compete together; they had died together, too.

JC, Summer's husband, and his younger brother, Samuel, had been on the way to a rodeo in Cheyenne, when a huge rig took them out. JC had died at the scene. Samuel died two days later in the hospital. Ivy couldn't imagine how awful it must have been for Melvin, losing his only children like that, or for Summer, being widowed with four young boys.

Scotch huffed in her ear, impatient to be out of the stall, and Ivy laughed, giving him a nudge with her shoulder to make him move so she could step around him. "You are so demanding," she said, exiting the stall. "I'll be back soon to take you out. Don't cause any trouble."

She set to work cleaning Scotch's tack, trying hard not to look at Belle's which she'd kept. Just seeing Belle's tack made her feel wistful. She missed her girl, but Ivy was also proud that she'd done something to help Ashley when others couldn't. Her mom would be proud, too. She had always done a lot to help others, especially in the Custer community.

"So many heavy sighs," Melvin Wyatt said, appearing at her side.

She pushed back her long braid and gave him a crooked smile. "Sorry. Didn't think anyone else was in here."

"I'm not bothered. But it sounds like you are." He folded his arms over his thick coat. "Feel like talking?"

"Just thinking about my mom. Wishing she were around. I still miss her a lot."

"She hasn't been gone that long."

"Two years."

"Took me a long time to accept that Nellie, my wife, was

gone, and then my boys. Nellie was sick, so I knew her death was coming. But the boys, that happened so fast. Didn't see it coming. Couldn't wrap my head around it. Didn't want to."

"Sam's named for your Samuel."

Melvin nodded. "JC and Samuel were best friends. Not at all surprised that JC named one of his boys after his brother."

"Are they much alike, Samuel and Sam?"

"No. Tommy reminds me a lot of Samuel. Samuel was full of fun, maybe too much fun. Laid back, easygoing, he loved to laugh and have a good time."

"That definitely doesn't sound like Sam."

"Sam's a man of his word. You can rely on him. Even if he isn't as social as his brothers, he's loyal and responsible. A solid family man."

Ivy liked Sam's grandfather. She liked him a whole lot. "Was he hurt when I broke up with him?"

"He's a private person, but we all knew it was a difficult time for him."

"I didn't think that would be it. I thought he'd come after me."

"Sam's blunt and straightforward. He probably thought you were serious and wanted out of the relationship."

A lump filled her throat and she looked away. "I don't even remember all the details anymore. So many things have happened since then."

"That's why it's good just to go forward. Looking to the past, wanting what's gone, it doesn't change anything, just makes it harder to accept the facts."

There were a dozen things she wanted to say, but didn't. Instead, she looked at the older man, remembering how she'd hoped he'd become her grandfather. She'd never had a grandfather. "Thank you for letting me come here," she said huskily. "I really do appreciate it."

"I know you do." He paused and gave her a faint smile, blue gaze warm. "Don't be too hard on yourself, Ivy. That also accomplishes nothing."

# CHAPTER SIX

S AM ENDURED A brief, but tense, conversation with his
mom before leaving the house to go find Ivy. His mom
could be ridiculous sometimes, and now was one of those
times, but he wasn't about to argue with her and upset the
whole family, just before Christmas, never mind Mom's
birthday in three days.

Sam found Ivy in the ring with Scotch, taking Scotch
through his paces. Scotch had an abundance of energy and
attitude this morning. His ears were forward, his tail was up,
and he wanted to go hard, but Ivy was holding back.

She needed to let him run, though. Scotch was full of
vim and vinegar, as Grandad would say, and the best way to
handle his excessive enthusiasm was to work him out.
Exhaust him a bit. But for some reason Ivy didn't look as
comfortable in the saddle as she normally did. He wondered
just how long it had been since she'd ridden him.

Sam grabbed a folding chair and turned it around, sitting
on it backward. Ivy had always been slim, but she looked
downright thin from a distance. He knew she watched her
weight so that she could remain competitive, but he suspect-

ed her thinness was due to stress rather than dieting.

Thinking of her being stressed made him think of Wes and thinking of Wes made Sam's temper spike. He seethed now, watching Ivy go round the ring, remembering her terrible little room at Joan's, as well as her hours at the bar. Sam hated her working at the Wolf Den, and not just because of Wes. She took the late shift and closed too many nights on her own. It just wasn't safe, and he wasn't the only one who felt that way. No one in his family approved, but that wouldn't make a good argument. Ivy, he knew from experience, didn't like being told what to do.

Ivy must have finally spotted him, because she turned Scotch his way, and cantered over.

"How long have you been sitting there?" she asked, breathing quickly, cheeks flushed, eyes bright.

"Not that long." Sam rose and closed the distance between them to scratch Scotch's forehead and then his cheek. When Sam stopped, Scotch shoved his muzzle into Sam's hand, demanding more.

"Scotch is greedy for attention today," Ivy said, shaking her head. "He's being a bit of a brat."

"He's glad to have you back," Sam answered. "He was practically two-stepping around the ring."

Ivy unzipped her chocolate-colored vest to cool down. "Oh yeah, he thinks he's the boss." She leaned forward to pat Scotch's neck. "But we're going to break you of that, big boy, aren't we?"

"Good luck," Sam answered. "It's a guy thing."

Ivy looked at Sam, lips curving, dark eyebrow arching. "Don't I know?"

Heat surged through Sam, heat and desire, along with a whole host of complicated emotions. At one point, Ivy had brought out the best in him, and then the breakup had brought out the worst, and he wasn't sure he ever wanted back on that roller coaster. Feelings were fine. Heartbreak wasn't. "Did you ever hear back from Ashley's parents?"

"I haven't checked my email this morning, but I can."

"Have you had breakfast?" he asked.

"No, just coffee."

"I was going to make some scrambled eggs. Want some?"

"Making bacon?"

"Are you making bacon?" he retorted.

She laughed. "I guess I am."

"What time do you work tonight?"

"I need to be there by five, but I wanted to stop by the garage before they close so they can get the repair started."

Sam knew if there ever was a time to press the issue about working at the Wolf Den, it was now. "You don't have to work at the bar, you know. We can find you work somewhere else."

"I owe George, though. He was good about giving me yesterday off."

"You don't owe George anything. And you don't owe Wes. And you don't owe me. You owe yourself, Ivy. It's time you put yourself first and took care of you. Working at the Wolf Den isn't good for you."

"It's not bad—"

"Answer me this, then. How would your mom feel about you working there?"

Ivy averted her face, chin lifting a fraction.

"Come on," he persisted. "The truth. How would she feel?"

"Doesn't matter," Ivy said lowly. "She's gone."

"She's with you still. She poured herself into you. Honor her by doing what's best for you."

Ivy swung her leg over Scotch's back and jumped down. "I have to work today. I won't leave George in the lurch."

"Can you give him notice today then? He can find others to work—" Sam saw she was about to interrupt and he continued firmly, "Even if he says he can't. He's owned that bar for twenty-some years. He knows how to find, and train, a new bartender, trust me." He held his hand out to her. "But first, how about those eggs?"

Ivy took a quick shower and headed back downstairs to a kitchen smelling of bacon and toast. "I thought I was going to help," she said, seeing that the eggs were scrambled and heaped in the skillet, bacon draining on a paper towel, and a stack of buttered toast on a plate.

"Sophie gave me a hand," Sam said, nodding toward the hall. "She saw me burning the first batch of bacon so she pitched in."

"You didn't have to do it all. You could have waited." Ivy reached for plates on the counter and handed him one. "Unless you're trying to rush off some place?"

"Not rush anywhere," Sam said, scooping eggs onto her plate and then his. "But there is something Mom talked to me about, and is hoping we'll do."

She'd just snagged a strip of bacon and munched on it. "What?"

He carefully added toast and bacon to his own plate before heading to the table. He set his plate down and then held a chair out for her.

She put her plate on the table and sat down. "What does she want us to do, Sam?"

"Move you down to Joe and Sophie's place."

Ivy frowned and lowered the next bite of bacon back to her plate. "This is about last night, isn't it?"

"She thinks we'll have less temptation if you're there."

"I'm not sleeping with you, Sam. Did you tell her that?"

"You don't say something like that to Mom. You just respect her rules and not make things more uncomfortable."

"So she hates me."

Sam laughed. "She doesn't hate you. She blames me. That's why she's moving you away from me."

"Maybe I should just move back to town."

"No." He wasn't even smiling anymore. "That's not an option."

"I feel so awkward."

"Don't. It's not a big deal, and Sophie's super excited you'll be staying at the house with them. She said you're their first guest."

AFTER BREAKFAST SAM moved all of Ivy's things from Joe's room down to Sophie and Joe's new house, while Sophie showed Ivy around the stylish log cabin she and Joe had built over the summer. It was a handsome two story with soaring beam ceilings and an open floor plan on the main level, the big kitchen opening to the great room with a long dining table in between. There were windows everywhere on all four sides and sunlight streamed in, the lovely winter light pooling on the wide plank floor.

Joe and Sophie had their own Christmas tree and wreaths hung in all the windows. Tall crimson pillar candles and more fresh green boughs covered the mantel. There were stockings hanging from the hearth, old-fashioned knit stockings with the names Joe and Sophie stitched on them. The whole house looked like something out of a magazine, beautiful, and elegant, rustic and luxurious at same time. Ivy exhaled, relaxing a little. Maybe staying here wouldn't be such a punishment after all.

Sophie continued the tour upstairs, showing Ivy a glimpse of the master bedroom and then a room down the hall that would one day be the nursery, and then another room at the far end of the hall that was their guest room.

The guest room featured a four-poster, rough-hewn log bed, with a thick red and white checked quilt. The shams were red and white as well, a mix of patterns that looked a little Scandinavian, and a whole lot of charming. More sunlight spilled through the tall windows giving her a view of trees and mountains and the dark blue Yellowstone River below.

Sophie crossed the floor and opened another door before flipping on the light. "Your own bathroom. It's got a tub and a shower, because Joe and I couldn't agree which was more important so, you have a little less closet, but you have more choices for bathing."

"This is wonderful," Ivy said huskily.

"So glad you like it. As I think Sam told you, you're our first guest."

"Will Sam's mom ever like me again?"

"She still likes you."

"I've been banished."

Sophie laughed. "I was banished, too. Sent down the mountain to Marietta."

"Were you really?"

"Yes. And I was given a very frosty reception for a long time."

"But you two get along so well now."

"You and Summer will be just fine. Trust me." And then Sophie wrapped her arms around Ivy, and gave her a big hug. "Just know I'm glad you're here." She drew back and smiled into Ivy's eyes, before letting go. "Those Wyatt boys can be challenging. I needed another girl on my team, and I didn't get just any girl, but one of the best barrel racers in the country."

"Somebody is doing too much talking," Ivy answered.

"I looked you up online, too. You've qualified twice for national finals in Las Vegas, the second time just two years ago. Apparently you were on fire."

"It was a good year. Competing, at least." Because it was also the year her mom died, and instead of being with her mom, she was traveling all over the country barrel racing.

"You'll be back in Las Vegas soon. Mark my words. You'll be there next year. And if you are, I want to go and watch you compete. I'm still kicking myself that I wasn't in Las Vegas to watch all the boys this year. It would have been awesome to see Sam get his first world title."

"Yeah." Ivy bundled her arms across her chest, and glanced around her room. "Can I please give you some money, to help cover some of the utilities while I'm staying here? I feel bad just crashing your place—"

"No! We don't want your money, and we won't take it. Even if you stayed for six months, we wouldn't charge you a single thing."

"I don't want to take advantage of you."

"You're not. You're a friend of Sam's, and we're glad to have you here."

"I don't know what to say."

"You said plenty. It's good to help friends." Sophie headed to the door. "Since Sam has brought everything over, I'll leave you alone to unpack and settle in. Shout if you need anything, okay?"

Then Sophie was gone and Ivy stood in the middle of her new room trying to decide what to unpack first. But honestly, she didn't feel like unpacking. She just wanted to get her truck and drive, and drive some more. It seemed as if she'd been locked down forever and she missed freedom and travel and the wide-open road.

A firm knock sounded on her open door and she glanced up. Sam stood in the doorway. "How are you doing?" he asked.

"Okay. How about you?"

"Thinking I might head out, do some Christmas shopping, grab lunch somewhere. Want to go with me?"

"Yes." She didn't even hesitate. "I was just thinking I need to go, get out, do something."

"Have you heard from Ashley's parents yet?"

"They're hoping I could come see Ashley tomorrow. Today she has a lot of physical therapy and they think she'll be too tired for a visit this afternoon."

"So you're free until work?"

She nodded. "I just want to stop by the garage, pay for my truck, and I'm free until work."

"When can you leave?"

"Let me just get my money and coat and we can leave

now."

"Meet you downstairs," he said, before leaving.

Ivy pulled her aluminum hatbox down from the closet shelf and opened it. It was empty. She didn't understand. Maybe she'd taken down the wrong hatbox. She took down the other one. Same.

She stared at the two open hat boxes on her bed. There was no mistake. Her money was gone. Every bill, whether a five, ten, twenty, or one hundred dollars, was gone.

Ivy dug through her empty duffel bag, and then checked her suitcase. She looked inside her boots. Checked drawers. Checked coat pockets. But nothing. Her money, all her savings, were gone.

She was still tearing her things apart when Sam returned. "Hey," he said, "thought we were heading out."

She sat back on her heels. "My money's gone," she choked. "Every bit of it."

"You're sure?"

"Yes. I kept it in my silver hatbox. And Sam, I had thousands saved. Over four thousand."

"When was the last time you saw it?"

"I counted it just a few days ago. Checking to see if I had enough for my truck, and I almost did. But now it's all gone."

"Did Joan have access to your room?"

"I would lock my door but I have a feeling she had a key. Sometimes things would be moved around a little bit, but I didn't think she knew about my money. I thought I'd hid it pretty well."

"This is why people use banks, Ivy."

"Thanks, Sam. Super helpful." She rose, and closed the open hatboxes and put them away on the closet shelf before folding the duffel bag and sticking that under her bed. "Go without me," she said lowly. "I can't pay off the truck now. There's no point in me going to Marietta."

"I'll pay for your truck, you pay me back."

"With what? Scotch? He's all I have left."

Sam's gaze met hers and held. "I know you're mad, but I'm not the enemy."

"No. I am! I'm an idiot—"

"Stop. Get your coat, get your purse, and whatever you'll need for work. We're getting out of here. Now."

As Ivy headed down the stairs with Sam, she caught a glimpse of Joe in the big open kitchen with Sophie. His arms were around his wife's waist, and he'd said something to make her laugh, and the next moment they were kissing.

She felt a pang seeing Joe and Sophie's happiness. Sam had noticed as well. "They're definitely in the honeymoon stage," Sam said, closing the front door behind them. "But it took some time for them to get there. They apparently had a rough start."

"Sophie said your mom was tough on her at first," Ivy said as they walked to Sam's truck parked next to the fleet of other trucks in the large gravel driveway. "I guess she made

Sophie stay in town?"

"I don't know much about that, but yeah, Mom wasn't thrilled Joe found his wife through an ad."

"But then he and Sophie fell in love."

"Thank goodness, because before Sophie arrived, Joe was a miserable sod. Last Christmas he was so irritable and unhappy none of us wanted to be around him, and this year, he's practically Father Christmas."

"It's sweet. I love how festive their house is," she said, climbing into the passenger side.

He closed the door behind her and then headed to the driver's side. "That's all Sophie's magic," he said, getting behind the wheel. "She went a little crazy there and here. She was the one that found our old stockings in the attic and got Joe to put up the big tree. She wanted Grandad and Mom to have a traditional Christmas when all the boys came home." Sam fell silent, and then turned to look at Ivy. "Think confronting Joan will do any good?"

Ivy shook her head. "She'll just deny it."

Sam started the engine and gave it a moment to warm up. "Has she taken things from you before?"

"Not outright steal, but she'd use things I'd bought and never replace them. Any food I put in the fridge was fair game."

"I'm really sorry."

"You didn't do anything wrong, Sam. You have no reason to apologize."

"I can be sorry this happened."

"True. Because I'm sorry, too."

"Let's go pay for your truck. We can figure out the logistics of paying me back later." He flashed a smile and shifted into reverse, backing up. "It's not as if I don't know where to find you."

"Very true." She hesitated. "And I'd appreciate the loan, if you really don't mind. I was so excited to get my truck again."

"I couldn't last a day without my truck. I get it." He shifted into drive and they headed past Sophie and Joe's and on down the Wyatt's private road.

"Sophie comes from a big family, doesn't she?"

"Yes. She loves to spoil Joe, and enjoys taking care of Mom and Grandad. Family is important to her."

Ivy felt an envious pang. The Wyatt house was never quiet. There was always something interesting happening. "Family is important to me, too. I just had a much smaller family."

"You and your mom were really close. I've never been close with my mom."

"That's probably because you prefer your own company."

"I do, some of the time." He shot her a quick glance. "But you're good company. Some of the best actually."

"Christmas at my house was so different from what you do at your house. We didn't have a big tree. We didn't have a lot of gifts."

"Did you have one of those tabletop trees?" he asked.

She nodded. "Yes, and all the ornaments were horse related. Every single one of them. I didn't think that was weird until now."

"What's weird about it? You were horse people, so of course you had a horse themed tree."

"When I was little I'd even set up a manger scene beneath the tree—with Joseph, Mary, baby Jesus in a wooden stable, surrounded by a dozen plastic horses. No sheep or cows or camels for me. Just horses keeping watch."

Sam laughed. "I know far more about you now than I did when we were together."

"We were always so focused on training, travel, and competing that it was tough finding time to just hang out and talk."

He didn't say anything and Ivy wondered if she shouldn't have said that. And just when she was certain she'd upset him, he said, "There's something to be said for just being friends… for just being yourself. Platonic relationships don't have all the added pressure of romantic ones."

Suddenly Ivy didn't know where to look, or what to do, or what to feel. There were moments—like this—where Sam felt like hers again, where she and Sam were comfortable and close, and they could talk about everything. "Speaking of romantic relationships, are you dating anyone right now?" she asked.

"I've been very casually dating," he answered, "but nothing that I'd call a relationship, and certainly nothing exclusive."

"So there's no girl who will be upset that I'm staying at your house over the holidays?"

"I've never cheated on you, Ivy, nor anyone else. That's not who I am."

"So our kiss last night…" She looked at him, hoping he'd jump in but Sam said nothing.

He lifted a brow, waiting.

Heat rushed through her, warming her face. "That kiss…"

"Yes?"

"It didn't feel… platonic."

"No?"

"No. It felt… amazing."

"Hmm. So less heat the next time? Maybe less tongue?"

Ivy burst out laughing. She reached over to slug Sam's arm. "Oh, my gosh. *Sam.*"

"What?" he asked innocently.

"Nothing," she spluttered, face hot, lips twitching because it was ridiculous how much she loved this Sam. He was everything to her. Still.

Heart tender, Ivy turned her head, focused on the scenery beyond the truck window, trying to control her chaotic emotions because she couldn't pretend that he didn't matter to her. She couldn't pretend that she didn't want what she had lost. Love.

Sam.

Sam's love.

A coyote suddenly darted across the road, and Sam braked, and then as it disappeared into the brush, he began driving again. They were descending back into the valley, and she watched the narrow road framed with clusters of aspens, oak, and pine. The Wyatt Ranch was high up in the Absaroka mountain range, their property nestled beneath the high, craggy peaks.

The Wyatts had a lot of land, beautiful land, with breathtaking views of the valley below. Even now she marveled at the beauty of Paradise Valley. "I'm a Montana girl through and through, but Paradise Valley is probably my favorite part of Montana. It's so beautiful, and I love being this close to Yellowstone. From Custer it was a three and a half hour drive. Here, you're just twenty minutes away."

"To the North Gate."

"Yes, but then it's an easy drive to Lamar Valley and the huge herds of buffalo."

"We could do that one day. Maybe after Christmas?" he suggested.

"Won't you be gone to close on your new place?"

"I'd only be gone a day. I'm not moving in immediately. The house on the property needs some work."

"So you're coming back here?"

He glanced at her, a smile in his blue eyes. "Do you

mind?"

She blushed again, everything inside of her all jangly and sensitive. "*No.*"

"We could train together, get ready for the new year."

Ivy crossed one leg over the other at the knee and wrapped her hands around her knee. "I'd do better working at the Wolf Den. I'd make money faster. I'm out of shape, and Scotch is out of shape. With my savings gone, I can't take any risks."

"If your money wasn't gone, what would you do?"

"I'd lease a place outside Marietta. I want a place with a barn and acreage."

"How many acres are you wanting?"

"At least ten. Twenty would be ideal."

"How many horses would you want to board and train?"

"The goal is eight or nine, but I'd be happy to start with four."

"You've crunched all your numbers?"

"I know this stuff. It's what Mom and I did together. I'm just going to do it on my own now." She hesitated. "I shouldn't have sold her business and rented her place out. I should have just settled down there and continued what she'd started."

"That's not what she would have wanted for you."

Ivy shrugged. "She loved watching me ride. She loved following my career, but it was never meant to be my whole life. I far prefer training over competing."

JANE PORTER

"Do you?"

"Competing is grueling. If you don't have a team, or family members who can travel with you and help out with everything, it's just too much."

"Wes used to travel with you."

She felt like she'd swallowed a rock. "Yes."

"It must have helped when he handled things, at least in the beginning?"

"It did. And it felt good to have him driving me, and helping make sure the horses were getting all the right veterinarian care, but it wasn't long before I discovered there was a price to be paid for having him help. I wasn't used to being told what to do. I wasn't used to being told to be quiet. I wasn't used to having someone decide which events I'd enter, and what horse I would ride—"

"He would do that?"

"That was probably the worst part of it. I know my horses, and I know where they'll do best, and when they'll do best. Belle's my girl, but like any mare, she can be moody, and there are times she shouldn't be competing. Same with Scotch, there are some places he just doesn't ride well at, and I know those places, and I know what Scotch needs to perform at his best."

"Wes is a cattle stock contractor. He knows nothing about horses."

"I know. But he read some magazines and talked to some folks and thought he was a hotshot." Ivy shrugged. "The worse thing I could do was contradict him in public. That always ended badly. Every single time."

"The moment you realized what you were dealing with, why didn't you just leave?"

She made a soft huffing sound. "I couldn't," she said even more quietly. "And I don't even know why. I was just… numb. Stuck."

"How did you finally make the break?"

"He had a big meeting in Denver. I was supposed to be heading to a rodeo in Texas. He put me in the truck, said he'd see me soon—"

"Because he was going to meet you after his meeting wrapped?" Sam guessed.

She nodded. "Once I hit the highway, I headed north instead of south, and kept driving through Utah and Idaho until I reached Polson. I spent a few days with Jill Snyder, the Montana Circuit Director, told her a little bit about my situation, and she helped me find the job at the Kruse ranch."

"So she knows about Wes?"

"She knows that I didn't want him to find me, and she knew that's why I wasn't going to be competing the rest of this year."

"She should have done more to help you."

"She did plenty. This was my problem, not hers."

THEY WERE NEARING Marietta and Sam took the exit off Highway 89 that was closest to the Wolf Den, as that was also where the garage was. Sam got out with Ivy, and then rather than go make the payment himself, he handed her his credit card. "Let me know if I'm needed," he said.

She nodded and disappeared inside the office.

Sam waited just outside, wanting to be available in case there was a problem, but at the same time not wanting to crowd her. Wes had done enough of that.

He looked over the rack of real estate and land brochures outside the garage. He picked up one and flipped through it, looking to see how much horse property in the area would cost. He'd never really priced property in Crawford or Park counties but knew this part of Montana was definitely more expensive than northeast, or east past Billings.

A couple ranches caught his eye. They were for sale, not lease, and one was huge and priced accordingly, and another was decently priced but it was hilly terrain and not suitable for horses. But there were a couple smaller places, places with both stables and barn. One that looked rather promising was just north of Livingston, and another on the way to Bozeman.

Maybe they should drive and visit both. Maybe there were a few other places they could check out, too. They really had nothing else to do today.

Ivy appeared, smiling. She handed him his credit card back. "Truck will be ready Tuesday before five. Thank you so much."

"Happy to do it."

"So, what do we do now?" she asked.

He flipped the glossy magazine over and showed her the cover. "How about we go check out some properties? Show me what you've been looking at, and maybe there are a couple in here you might find interesting."

"I don't think those are for lease."

"No, but it'd be interesting to see what a place would cost, if you wanted to buy some day."

"I do like it here," she agreed. "But I won't have enough to buy here, not for years."

"You would if you sold your mom's place."

A tiny muscle pulled in Ivy's jaw and emotion darkened her eyes. "I've thought about that, but I don't know. It's really all I have left of her."

"Then why don't you live there?"

"Because I'd be lonely. I haven't lived in Custer in years. And then I've my tenants. It's a long-term lease."

"How long? Ten years? Twenty?"

"No. I think it's four."

"So you still have two years left on the lease, and then you could live there."

She looked away, her gaze sweeping the Gallatin Range with prominent Copper Mountain in the foreground. "Custer was fine growing up, but it's not Marietta." She looked back at Sam. "Little by little, this place has started to feel like home." The corners of her mouth lifted. "I never anticipated wanting to stay here, but helping Ashley, and working with Hope, and then coaching Kat after school—"

"Whose Kat?"

"A student at Marietta High. She loves horses and wanted to know more about barrel racing, not sure if it would be something she'd like. So I worked with her a couple times a week for a month, introducing her to the sport."

"What did she decide?"

"That it wasn't for her, and she's glad she found out before she invested too much more time or money into it."

"How much did you charge per hour?"

Ivy blushed. "I didn't."

"Why not?"

"Her parents offered, but I didn't want money. I just wanted to help her. It feels good to contribute, you know?"

"Your time is valuable, Ivy. It's okay to charge for it—"

"I know, and I will. Once I have my place, I most definitely will. Right now, I'm just building relationships. Making a name for myself."

"I won't argue with that." He handed her the real estate magazines. "See if there's any place in one of these that would be worth a look. I'd be fun to just drive around, pretend we're shopping."

"You've already done your shopping."

"But you haven't, and I love land. Why not have some fun?"

They spent two hours driving, checking out properties listed in the magazines, as well as other properties they found online. They didn't actually go inside any of the houses or barns, but they drove back roads, frontage roads, and down quite a few private roads to get a feel for the property, its boundaries, its access, as well as neighbors. There were some places that didn't appeal at all, and there were others that made Ivy's expression light up as she scribbled notes into a tiny notebook in her purse.

"What are you writing down?" Sam asked her at one point.

"Just the stuff I like, or the stuff I'd like to have at my place." She held up one of the magazines with a full-page ad. "Like this place, I love everything about this place. I'd lift it up and set it down here if I could."

"Where is it?"

"Clyde Park."

"That's not that far."

"It's not Marietta. I want to be part of the community, the way my mom was part of Custer."

"So what does this place near Clyde Park have that you like?"

"*Everything*. Flat acreage, state-of-the-art stable for twenty horses, full indoor barn with heated wash racks, cross ties with stall mats, full tack room, wash/dryer, lounge room with viewing window to indoor arena, restroom, and a manager's office." She looked up at Sam, awed. "Imagine.

How amazing is that?"

"But no outdoor training space?"

"Let me keep reading. A huge outdoor arena with deep sand footing, plus a horse car wash."

"What about the house?"

"Four bedrooms, four and a half bath, three-car garage plus a separate garage for trucks and trailers."

"How much?"

She laughed. "*Millions.*"

"How many millions?"

"Too much to even think about, but I love so much of what they've done here, and I could do that over time to my place, when I have one. I just need the right land at the right price—" She broke off as her phone rang. Ivy reached into her purse to retrieve it. It was Ashley's mom calling. Ivy answered. "This is Ivy," she said.

"Ivy, it's Lisa Howe. Is there any way you could come see Ashley today? She's really upset and she won't talk to me, and she won't work with her physical therapist."

"What happened?"

"She wanted to see her horse, and so we pushed her wheelchair out to the stable, and once there, she wouldn't leave. She just started crying and won't stop." Lisa's voice broke. "I'm so worried. I don't know how to calm her down."

"I'll head there now," Ivy said, glancing at Sam. He nodded at her. "We're just north of Livingston, in Grannis, so it'll take us about forty-five minutes but we're coming."

"Thank you."

Ivy hung up and drew a deep breath.

Sam reached over and took her hand. "I heard a little bit of that," he said. "Ashley's mom?"

"Ashley loves horses the way I love horses," Ivy said.

"Paraplegics can ride horses. There are quite a few programs that use riding as a means of therapy."

"And there is adaptive equipment, too. I remember reading years ago about engineering students at University of Utah designing assistive tech for spinal cord injured riders. But Ashley's injury is still very recent, and her parents are afraid, probably overprotective, about allowing Ashley into the saddle again."

Sam shot her a knowing look. "You disagree."

"I think if Ashley needs to be in the saddle, you put her in the saddle. I've looked up what needs to be done. She'd probably need a seat belt attached to the saddle, as well as some straps, or Velcro, to attach her legs to the stirrups, but on the right horse, she could do very well."

"As a paraplegic, does she have sufficient core strength?"

"It's one of the things they would have worked with her on at her rehab facility. Core strength and balance is essential to everything. From what I was reading, the only way to develop that strong core is for her to strengthen existing neural connections and gain muscle memory by regeneration of new connections."

Sam wasn't surprised by Ivy's knowledge, but he was impressed. When Ivy was passionate about something, she put her whole heart into it. "You've been doing a lot of research then."

"I've been following Ashley since before the injury. She was an outstanding junior barrel racer. She had a big future before the accident—"

"What did happen? It was a farm accident, but what specifically happened?"

"It was a freak accident. She was driving a tractor, plowing a field for her dad, and the tractor flipped, sending her flying. She broke her back in the fall."

Sam asked nothing more.

THEY REACHED THE Howe's in Belgrade just after one. Ivy introduced Sam to Ashley's parents before Lisa walked Ivy out to the barn to Ashley. Ivy stopped Lisa just before they reached the barn. "I've got this," Ivy said. "Let me talk to her on my own."

"She might not be very nice."

"That's okay. If I were in her shoes, I wouldn't be very nice, either."

Ivy continued on her own the rest of the way to the barn. "Ashley, it's Ivy Wyckoff," Ivy called out as she approached the open barn door. "Can I come in?"

"No." The voice was muffled and scratchy.

"Can I talk to you from here?"

"Did my parents call you?"

"Yes."

"Then go away. Because I know what they want you to say. They want you to tell me that it's unrealistic for me to ever really ride again, and that competing is out."

"They might want me to say that," Ivy answered, zipping up her coat and folding her arms over her chest. "But that's not what I would ever tell you. And that's not what I planned to tell you tomorrow when I was going to come see you."

There was silence for a long minute, before Ashley hiccupped. "No?"

Ivy felt a pang for Ashley. "No." She added, "Because I don't agree with them."

"You don't?"

"No."

More silence. And then, "Would you help me ride again?"

"Yes."

Another beat of silence. "Ivy?"

"Yes, love?"

"You can come in."

A lump filled Ivy's throat and she blinked as she entered the barn. It took a second for her eyes to adjust to the dim lighting in the barn, and then she spotted Ashley on the ground, and the wheelchair next to her, on its side. Ashley had drug herself into a sitting position and Ivy took a seat on the ground next to the girl.

For a little bit no one said anything.

"It's cold," Ashley said, with a shiver.

"I think a storm is moving in," Ivy answered. "We're supposed to get a lot of snow Sunday or Monday."

Ashley pushed golden-brown bangs off her forehead. Her eyes were puffy, her face blotchy "I hate my wheelchair. I hate that I can't walk. I hate that everyone looks at me funny at school now."

"Maybe they're just sorry you got hurt?"

"But they don't look at me the way they used to. They look at me and then away, really fast, as if they didn't see me. As if I'm not really there."

"I bet your friends don't."

"I don't have any friends anymore."

"It might not seem like it, but I bet you do. It's just been hard with you away so long."

"But I can't go out and do stuff with them like I used to. They have parties and sleepovers and I'm not invited."

"Maybe they think you couldn't manage at their house? Maybe they're worried they have steps and your wheelchair couldn't get up them, or that their bathroom is too small—"

"How do you know this stuff?"

"My mom had a really good friend in Custer who was in a wheelchair. She got hurt in a car accident and was left paralyzed. She was a single mom like my mom, and so we did things together. Some holidays we'd go see her, and other times she and her kids would come to our house. It gave me a chance to see how she did things."

"She was a mom?"

Ivy nodded. "She had three kids."

"And she could take care of them?"

"Even in a wheelchair, yes."

"Did she drive them places?"

"Yes, and she cooked for them, and did their laundry, and dropped them off at school before going to work."

"Did she drive one of those big vans, or a real car?"

"It was a real car. It just had hand controls so she'd accelerate and brake using her hands, not her feet."

Ashley thought about this for a little bit. "I want a truck. I've always wanted a truck, that way I can still pull my horse and do all the things I want to do."

"I don't see why you can't do that."

"Where would my wheelchair go? If there's no one to help me?"

"If my mom's friend, Cindy, was alone, she'd lean her car seat back and put the wheelchair over her shoulder, behind her." Ivy smiled at her. "You know, you've got an advantage over a lot of girls. You already have a really great core from riding. You just have to keep your strength up, and working on your balance."

Ashley looked up at her. "When can I ride again?"

"Want me talk to your parents?"

Ashley nodded. "And then I want to train. I want to compete again. I might not be great, but I can try."

"Yes, you can."

"Will you help me?"

"I will."

"And help me barrel race?"

"I'll talk to your parents."

"They'll say no."

Ivy shrugged. "Leave them to me. I might have some information that will help them think differently. But what if we keep that as our secret for now, and just work on getting you back in the saddle?"

"When?"

"How about after Christmas? That will give me time to check out different saddles and see if there is any special adaptive equipment we need. I want to make sure we're successful, otherwise your parents will just get worried, and we don't want them worried. We want them on our team, yes?"

"Yes." Ashley shivered. "It's cold."

"Want to get back in your chair?"

"How come you're the only one that doesn't call it a wheelchair."

Ivy laughed. "Because Cindy never called it a wheelchair, just a chair, or her chair." She reached over and smoothed Ashley's long ponytail. "How do you want me to help you? What's best?"

"Normally I'm supposed to use something to help me push up, but I think I'm too cold." Ashley's brow furrowed and she looked anxiously at Ivy. "Do you think you could lift me into my chair? Just this once?"

"Absolutely. Not a problem." Ivy got to her feet, and righted the wheelchair before crouching next to the girl. "Put your arm around my neck. That's it. Here we go."

Ashley was light, far lighter than some of the hay bales she'd had to muscle in her lifetime, and Ivy was able to get her into the wheelchair without much effort.

Ashley wiggled, finding her balance and then adjusted her legs. "I guess I have to go face my parents," she said, wrinkling her nose. "We had a huge fight."

"They love you so much, I'm sure they've already forgiven you."

"I know they love me, but I get so mad at them. They just hover all the time."

"This is hard for them, too. They wish they could make all this go away and they can't."

Ashley's eyes filled with tears. "My dad says that all the time. He says he wishes it was him who got hurt. That it should have been him. But I'm glad it wasn't him. I don't know that he could do this. But I can."

For a second Ivy couldn't breathe, her chest hot and tender, and then she leaned down and hugged Ashley fiercely. "Yes, you can," she whispered. "You've got this. Just keep fighting. And I'll fight with you, okay?"

Ashley hugged her back. "Okay."

They emerged from the barn, Ivy walking next to Ashley as she rolled herself slowly over the uneven ground toward her parents and Sam. And then she got a look at Sam and let out a yelp. "Is that Sam Wyatt?"

Ivy grinned. "Yes."

"Oh, my gosh. Can I get his autograph?"

Ivy laughed. "I'm sure he'd be happy to give it to you."

# CHAPTER SEVEN

Leaving the Howes in Belgrade, Ivy and Sam headed back toward Marietta, stopping for a late lunch in Bozeman. There wasn't a lot of conversation at first, both contemplative. It wasn't until they'd finished their sandwiches that Sam asked about what took place in the barn.

Ivy handed her empty plate to the waitress and then looked at Sam. "Ashley's a teenage girl wanting to believe she's going to have a normal life, and I did my best to assure her that she could, and that she would."

"And riding?"

"I want to get her a saddle, one that would allow her to ride, and potentially race. There's got to be some out there, but until we find the right one, I need to come up with something that would let her ride after Christmas. That's when I've promised to return and start working with her."

"Don't you think you need to talk to her parents, get their permission? Her dad seems pretty adamant that they protect her—"

"It's a little late for that, isn't it?" Ivy interrupted hotly. "She's already hurt. Her life's been permanently changed.

Don't hold her back. Let her challenge herself. Let her dream."

Sam held up his hands. "I'm not the one you've got to convince. I just know what he said while you were in there, talking to Ashley."

"The way I see it is, they either get behind her and make her dreams possible or they use fear to break her spirit." Ivy tapped the side of her water glass, a restless drumming that revealed her tension. "What would you do, if she was your daughter? Would you let her compete again?"

"It's a dangerous sport."

"Preaching to the choir."

"But most sports have an element of risk. Athletes in every sport get injured. I think about football—Grandad had all of us playing when we were growing up—and now they talk about the lasting damage from concussions, and it might only take one really bad hit to have permanent damage."

"Right. So, what would you do if Ashley was your baby girl and she wanted to get back into her favorite sport?"

Sam stared off across the restaurant, his blue eyes narrowed, deep creases at his eyes. "I'd put her on the horse myself," he said, turning to look at Ivy. "And drive her to every single rodeo she wanted to enter."

"What about your career?"

He shrugged. "I'd be happy to give it all up, if it'd allow me to support my daughter."

❦

THEY REACHED MARIETTA with a half hour before she needed to start work, and Sam asked if she'd mind if they stopped at the western wear store on Main Street as he wanted her input on his mom's birthday gift. "I want to get her a vest, something warm and comfortable that she could wear around the house."

"I don't know her taste, but I'm happy to help," she answered.

Inside the store, Sam pulled out a couple different vests and asked Ivy what she thought. Ivy even modeled a few of them for him. "This collar's too high," she said about one. "I'd find it annoying if every time I turned my head, it brushed my chin."

"What about that quilted ivory one? It's not really thick, but do you think it'd keep her warm?"

Ivy put it on, zipped the black zipper. The vest hit lower than some, reaching mid hip. "I like that it's got a little style, with the black piping." She slid her hands into the pockets, which were nice and deep. "The pockets are good, too. You could keep a packet of tissue in them, or a key, or even gloves if need be. I actually like this one at lot."

"I hear a but, though."

"I'm not sure it's your mom. She doesn't wear a lot of ivory or black. She seems to prefer blues, lavender, and sometimes a soft pink." Ivy went to the rack and pulled out a vest that was almost an antique rose. "I think this color would look really pretty on her."

"The zipper's gold."

"It's a feminine vest." Ivy took off the ivory vest and slid her arms into the pink one. "But look, it's not bulky, and it has great pockets and the armholes are wide enough that they won't limit her movement."

"I'm going to get it."

"I think she'll love it." And then Ivy leaned in to him for a kiss, before realizing just what she was doing. She stopped short of actually touching him, but it was obvious what she'd almost done. "Oops." She forced a smile. "Looks like I'm getting a little too comfortable with you."

"I've kissed you. Twice. I wouldn't complain if you kissed me once."

"But the kisses are confusing. I'm not sure what they mean."

"I think it means we like each other."

She turned away, her gaze sweeping the store. "Is there anything else you want to buy while we're here? I still have a few minutes before I have to be at work."

"You don't want to talk about us?"

"We have ten minutes before I start working. I really don't think now is a good time."

"Then tomorrow let's talk. Maybe we can go for a ride, get away from the house, and discuss what happened two years ago, because I have questions—"

"So do I."

"Great, then we'll finally be able to clear some things

up."

❦

VEST PURCHASED, SAM drove Ivy to the Wolf Den as the first streetlamps came on. It wasn't yet five but already dark. Dirty mounds of snow marked the bar's entrance, making the eyesore of a building look even more bedraggled.

"You can just drop me here," she said.

"I'm coming in," he answered.

She scanned the parking lot for Wes's big red shiny truck. "I don't see his truck."

"He could have walked. He could have hidden it. He could have a different set of wheels."

Sam parked in one of the spots and turned off the engine. "I'm not taking any chances, nor should you."

"I'm not."

"Good. Then you shouldn't object to me hanging out tonight," he said, swinging his door open and stepping out, boot crunching ice.

"I do feel a little guilty taking up your whole night," she said, opening her own door. "You should go home, spend the evening with your family, and then come back at closing time to get me."

"What if Wes shows up and makes things ugly?"

"I'll take a barstool and crack him over the head."

Sam gave her a long look. "Seriously."

"Lucy's working tonight and she always carries Mace. I'll

just Mace him."

"You'll Mace Wes?"

The wind grabbed at her ponytail, the long strands flying in every direction. "If I have to."

"That's good to know."

She stepped in front of him, put a hand on Sam's chest to stop his progress. "Go watch a Christmas movie with your mom, and then come back at eleven, and then hang out with me. But please don't just abandon her, not when she's so glad to have you at the ranch this time of year."

"Mom understands I'm concerned about you. We're all concerned about you."

"I appreciate that, I do, but no one in that bar will let anything happen to me. We're like a family, a really colorful, dysfunctional family, but we look out for each other."

"How about this? I come in, have one beer, and maybe a bite of something, and then if all is well, I'll go home, and then come back at ten or eleven, and keep an eye on things until you close."

"Won't you be bored?"

"No. Food, drink, and even free entertainment."

Ivy went hot all over. "You mean the dancers."

Sam's expression was innocent as he opened the door for her. "I was referencing the TV over the bar. The one perpetually turned to The Weather Channel."

"Hmph," she answered, marching inside.

"Ivy's here," Lucy sang out as Ivy crossed the middle of

the floor, heading toward the bar. Hank, the weekend day bartender worked part-time and went to college at night, high-fived her on his way out.

"Have I missed anything?" Ivy asked Lucy, putting her things away, and then washing her hands.

"Nope. It's been pretty quiet. I think everyone's out shopping, getting ready for Christmas." Lucy looked over at Sam, where he'd taken a stool at the counter. "You're Tommy's brother."

"I am," Sam answered. "Didn't you used to have red hair?"

"I did. What do you think of the pink?" Lucy asked, swiveling her head right to left, showing off the fluorescent hue.

"I like it. Suits you," he said.

She grinned, and extended a hand. "Lucy Truly. Tommy and I went to school together. We were boyfriend and girlfriend in first grade. Pretty serious relationship."

Sam laughed and shook her head. "Sam Wyatt, and it's nice to meet you, Lucy Truly."

"That is my real name, in case you're wondering," she said. "I don't know what my parents were thinking." She noted activity across the bar. "Better go, but I'll be back."

After Lucy walked away, Sam glanced at Ivy. "She's the one with the Mace?"

Ivy nodded.

"I have a feeling she wouldn't be afraid to use it," he said.

169

"No. You don't mess with Lucy. She's fearless. She might look all soft and fluffy, but she studied criminal justice at University of Montana, and is preparing now for law school."

Sam turned to look at Lucy waiting on some customers. "I wonder if Tommy remembers her."

"He couldn't take his eyes off of her the night of his friend's birthday, but we both know Tommy is a flirt."

"How did Lucy respond?" Sam asked.

"She didn't give him the time of day," Ivy answered, before heading down to the other end of the counter.

SAM PASSED THE hour by picking at the nachos Ivy served him—probably the worst nachos he'd ever had in his life—and washing them down with the beer. At least the beer was cold. He was just about to leave when the door opened and Wes walked in.

Sam saw the moment Ivy registered Wes's arrival, even as she glanced from Wes to Sam, and back again.

She didn't look afraid tonight. If anything she looked determined. Resolute.

She stopped in front of him, and this time she didn't offer to refill his drink or get him anything else to eat. "You can go now," she said quietly. "I've got this."

"I'm not comfortable leaving you."

"Maybe not, but you made me a promise and I want you

to keep it."

"That was before Wes arrived."

"It doesn't matter if he's here or not. We agreed that while I work, you'd spend the evening with your family. That was our arrangement, and I expect you to stick with it."

"I don't want you afraid—"

"I'm not afraid, and tonight Wes won't harass me. I'm done being intimidated, by him, or by anyone."

Ivy was silent a moment. "Lucy made me realize I've allowed Wes to bully me. I didn't put a stop to it sooner, but I have now, and he needs to hear from me, that we're done, and he has no more power over me."

"And if he lays a hand on you?"

"I'll scream bloody murder, call the sheriff, call you, call Tommy and Billy, call Joe—" She broke off, smiled. "See? I'm going to be okay. You've given me the kick in the pants I needed."

"Can you come around the counter?" Sam asked.

She did, and he put his hands on her hips and pulled her toward him. "There are things I'd rather do than kick you in the pants."

She laughed, and blushed. "I hope they're one of the things I enjoyed."

"Well, they're certainly one of the things I enjoyed."

Her blush deepened and she looked away. "You're making it hard to concentrate on work."

"Then I'll leave, but promise me you will call if you need

me."

Her eyes locked with his, and she looked deep into the blue depths for a long moment. "I promise."

Sam kissed her forehead, and then her lips, a long bone-melting kiss before he rose from his stool and walked out.

Ivy waited for the door to close behind Sam, and then she exhaled, and drew another breath, trying to clear her head, and steady her pulse. Once she was calm, and fully in control of her emotions she walked down the counter to confront Wes.

"Hello, beautiful," he said, giving her the smile that she now knew was as plastic and fake as anything.

She didn't bother smiling back. "I don't want you here," Ivy said bluntly. "I'd like you to leave."

She'd clearly caught Wes off guard. He looked surprised, even shocked, and then his expression changed, and he summoned back the charming smile, the one that now made her skin crawl. "We can't be friends?"

"No."

Her blunt answer seemed to throw him again, but he recovered his smile, although he looked slightly less sure of himself. "Not sure why you just disappeared on me. I was worried sick. Spent months trying to find you, trying to make sure you were okay."

"As you can see, I'm okay."

"How long have you been here in Marietta?"

"It doesn't really matter, Wes. It's none of your business,

not anymore."

"You and Sam really together? Back with your old boy-friend? Or is it just an act?"

"Not an act. I love him. I've always loved him." She forced herself to meet Wes's gaze. "Even when I was with you, I loved him."

Wes's smile faded. His brown gaze hardened. "You're telling me I was playing second fiddle?"

"I'm telling you what I should have told you in the beginning. That my heart was taken. There's only ever been one man for me, and that's Sam Wyatt."

"So where was he, when you needed him? Where was he when your mom died? Ivy, I was there. I picked up those pieces. Hell, you were in pieces. You were a mess—"

"Yeah, I was. And you were more than happy to take control of all those pieces, to take control of me."

"And look what I did for you. Look what I did for your career. Sam never helped you. He didn't ever put you, or your career, first. But I did. The year we were together you earned twice as much as what you'd ever earned. I doubled your income. I took you from being a good barrel racer and I made you a star—"

"Wes, hold up. Come on. You've been drinking the Kool-Aid if that's what you think. Yes, you doubled my income, but I'm not a star—"

"I made everyone want you. I got your face everywhere."

"I never wanted that. I never asked for any of that. You

never once consulted with me, you just took over and told me where to go, and what to do, and if I protested, you got ugly."

"I lost my temper a couple of times, and I'm sorry about that, I should have been more patient, but Ivy, you didn't seem to appreciate everything I was doing for you, and all the money we were making."

"Let's talk about money, Wes." Ivy knew Lucy was waiting for her but Lucy was just going to have to wait a few minutes longer. "Where is the money? Where is my money? If I have so much, why am I deeply in debt?"

"You're not in debt."

"My credit cards are full. You never paid them down."

"A mistake," he said. "Because you have money in your checking account, and the rest, of course, has been invested."

"I'm closing all of those accounts," Ivy said. "And I want you to hand over information on all of my investments, too. We're through. You're not my manager, you're not my friend, you're not my boyfriend. You're nothing to me. I want you out of my life and I'm letting everyone who ever worked with me know that you're not part of my career, and that any agreement made with you does not hold up. I will take you to court if I have to. I'm taking my name back, my career back, and all the control."

"So much self-confidence. I'm impressed. Let me applaud Wyatt for doing wonders for your self-esteem."

"This isn't about Sam. It's about me. I don't need a man

to fix me. I was hurt, but never broken, and it just took me a little time to figure out it's okay to fall and to fail. What's not okay is giving up." She glanced past him to the door where the big burly bearded bouncer was standing. Ivy's gaze met the bouncer's just long enough so that he would know she was checking in with him, alerting him to potential trouble.

And then she looked back at Wes, who looked by turns, angry and miserable. "Sam's coming back in a bit, and I wouldn't be here when he gets back. I wouldn't ever come around again. I don't want you around. Sam most definitely doesn't want you around. So why don't you head on out, get in your truck, and leave Marietta once and for all."

Wes stared at her, mouth tight, jaw set. "Just tell me this. Is it true you're engaged? Because I don't see a ring on your finger."

She arched a brow to hide her surprise. "I don't think it's any of your business."

"I'd just think if Wyatt was that serious, he'd put a ring on your finger. Unless, you take it off when he's not around?"

"Again, what Sam and I do is none of your business."

Wes rose, shoving his stool back with a loud scrape. "Then tell him to stop texting me about your wedding. Even if you did invite me, I wouldn't come."

Ivy watched Wes walk out, and then headed down the bar to get the drinks together for Lucy. "Sorry about that," she apologized to Lucy. "That needed to be done."

"Not a problem," Lucy answered. "I grabbed a couple of long necks. I'll take these over and then come back for the rest."

❦

SAM WATCHED EXACTLY one Christmas movie with his mom and family before bolting out the door and returning to town.

He arrived back at the Wolf Den well before ten. He sat for a moment, telling himself to chill out, before he walked in. He spotted some of the real estate magazines on the floor of the passenger seat and scooped them up to look through once he went inside.

Entering the bar, he nodded at the bouncer, and then went to his favorite barstool which was happily empty. Ivy gave him a look from the other end of the bar but he wasn't sure how to decipher it. He wouldn't call Ivy a hothead, but she definitely wore her heart on her sleeve, far more than other women he'd dated. But that was also one of the things he'd always liked about her. Her warmth. Her energy. Her passion.

He pulled the real estate magazines from his coat pocket and flipped through the ones he hadn't yet looked at. Lots of big houses, and some smaller ones, but nothing really suitable for what Ivy wanted. And then just as he started to close the magazine he saw an ad that read, *Paradise Valley*

*Montana Horse Facility, Home, Arena & More.*

He skimmed the description. *Located in the heart of Paradise Valley, 26 miles to Yellowstone Park, 1/4 mile to Yellowstone River, this is a must-see property for the horse-lover.*

Twenty-one acres.

A completely remodeled house with three bedrooms and two baths with outdoor living and three-hundred-sixty-degree views of mountains and valley.

Sam glanced up at Ivy, who was still not making any effort to come speak to him. "Can I get a drink?" he asked.

She leaned against the counter and gave him a frosty look "No."

"Why not?" he asked.

"I don't like this game you're playing with Wes. I don't want to be part of it."

Okay, interesting. "Which part?"

Her arms folded over her chest. "The part where you say outrageous things just to piss him off."

"What's outrageous?"

"Oh, maybe the part about us being engaged, the part about sending him an invite to the wedding."

He bit the inside of his cheek to keep from smiling. "You didn't like that?"

"No. It was humiliating."

"How was it humiliating?"

"None of it's true." She held up one hand, wiggled her fingers. "He asked about my ring. Wanted to know where it was. That was awkward. Maybe you should have warned me."

"Did it work? Is he gone?"

"I didn't need to tell him a lie to make him leave. I could just tell him the truth. And I did—"

"Did you tell him we aren't engaged?"

"No. I told him I wanted him out of my life. I made it clear he wasn't involved in my career anymore. He wasn't my manager, or my friend, and he needed to leave, and never bother me again."

Sam felt a rush of protective pride. Good girl. That couldn't have been easy for her. "Proud of you."

"I can handle myself."

"I didn't say you couldn't."

She gave him another long look. "You can't tell people we're engaged if it's not true. It's not okay."

"I'm sorry."

Ivy sighed. "What do you want to drink?"

"Just a water."

"That's it?"

He nodded. "But check this out. You might like this place. It sounds like it would be perfect for you."

"What makes it so perfect?" she asked.

"It's not far from here. It has twenty-one acres. A nice house, as well as a second cabin on the property that could serve as a bunk house or vacation rental property."

She carried the water over and set it down in front of

him. "What else?"

"Small animal pens, barn, huge shop for cars and garage."

"Only the barn interests me."

"Private air strip adjacent to property," he added.

"I don't care about that."

Sam smiled. "How about the indoor arena, stable with tack rooms, eight stalls, vet room, wrangler's quarters?"

"You're talking my language now."

"Outdoor arena," he added, glancing down to read, "Plus ten individually fenced paddocks, all with auto waterers."

He could see from her expression she really liked everything he was saying. "How does the house look?"

"Reminds me of your mom's house in Custer. A single-story ranch. Attractive but not overly fancy."

Ivy held her hand out for the magazine and he gave it to her. "It does look a little like Mom's," she said, before inhaling sharply. "Sam, it's still over a million."

"You could offer less, get it for maybe a million."

Ivy's eyes suddenly filled with tears. "You don't get it, do you? I don't have a million dollars. I don't even have a trailer anymore. Why tease me like that? I'm not you. I don't rake in a quarter of a million dollars in one week in Vegas. It takes me an entire year to earn two hundred thousand, and that's in my best year ever, riding three or four rodeos a weekend, *and* placing high in Vegas. My best year is your average year, and maybe that's why my career never was as important as yours—"

"I have never said that."

"Maybe not in words, but in actions. You entered the rodeos best for you. It was always what was best for you." And then she dropped the magazine and walked off.

Sam wrestled with her words, first confused, then angry, and then perplexed again. Is that how she thought it was? Is that really what she believed? He'd never not considered her? She was wrong. Because he'd never thought his career was more important. Yes, he did make more money, but he needed to make more money, especially if he was going to provide for a family. Ivy wouldn't be able to compete when pregnant, and there would be years she couldn't travel when they had babies, so yes, he needed to be the primary bread-winner but it wasn't to marginalize her, it was to reassure her that he was planning for the future. Their future.

Unfortunately, Ivy didn't give him a chance to talk about any of this as she avoided him for the rest of the night. Sam killed time by watching the weather reports—snow was coming, possibly a lot of snow—and checking news on his phone, and flipping through the remaining magazines.

When Ivy was finally free to leave, they walked out to-gether but she was still giving him the silent treatment as they climbed into his truck and set off south on Highway 89 for Pray and the Wyatt Ranch.

Ivy didn't seem inclined to start a conversation so Sam dove straight in. "I have never once treated you like a second-class citizen."

"I'm tired, Sam. I don't want to talk about it tonight because we'll just end up in another fight."

"Just explain one thing to me. How did I humiliate you by reaching out to Wes?"

"First, you went behind my back and texted him. Not okay. And second, you made up stupid stuff about us being engaged—"

"How is that humiliating?"

"How is it not? I would have killed to hear just one of those things when we were dating. I would have loved a ring... a proposal... a wedding. I would have loved your undivided attention, but I never got it. Not for a day, never mind a week."

Sam swore under his breath.

"I heard that," she said.

"Good, because this is absurd."

"It's not absurd, and this, what we're talking about right now, is why we broke up—"

"*I* didn't break up with you," he corrected.

"No, I broke up with you because I wanted to be important to you and I was tired of trying to get your attention. Your horses got more attention than I did. Your brothers got more attention. Heck, the rodeo clowns got more attention, too."

He wasn't sure if he should laugh or not. "Now you're just being dramatic, and if it makes you feel better, go ahead, because after everything Wes has put you through, you're entitled to let off a little steam."

Ivy stomped one boot on the floorboard. "You're giving me permission to be upset? You're giving me permission to have feelings? That's so good of you, Sam. *Thank you.*"

"That wasn't what I meant, and you know it. I would never disrespect you. Not ever."

Sam was so angry his jaw ached from grinding his back molars so hard. "And I definitely wasn't trying to make you feel bad by telling you about the horse property near Livingston. I thought you'd like it. I thought it was something within your reach."

"A million dollars? Sam, I've got nothing."

"I don't think it's that bad. Wes made it sound like you have some investments left. Maybe not as much as you should but apparently you're not destitute."

"How do you know?"

"I made Wes tell me."

"What specifically did he say?"

"That he's bought some stocks and bonds for you..." He made a face. "But he made some bad investments, too." Sam glanced at her. "The good news is that you also have your mom's place. Once you sell that property, you'll be able to afford something you like."

"But that's still a couple years away."

"Unless you could get your renters to leave."

"How do I do that?"

"Give them an incentive. Make an offer they can't refuse."

"Which would cost more money." She closed her eyes, held her breath. "I'm sorry for yelling at you. Sorry I said mean things."

"What happened to your trailer?"

She slunk lower in her seat. "One of the ranch hands at Kruse's backed into it, crushing it."

"Did the guy reimburse you? Buy you a new trailer?"

"He was also laid off. Where is he going to find the money to pay me back?"

"Did you even ask?"

"He felt bad. I didn't want to make him feel worse."

"Ivy, you can't always put everyone first. You've got to start putting yourself first."

"If it had been Kruse, I would have asked for compensation, but Davey had nothing."

Sam made a rough exasperated sound deep in his throat.

She glanced at him. "What?"

"Nothing."

"No, say it. I want to know what you're thinking."

Sam knew that if he was honest, they were just going to end up fighting, but not being honest wasn't right, either. "I'm thinking Wes got his claws into you because you're so open, and too generous. You're too quick to put others first. You have to put yourself first. You have to do what is best for you."

"Like you do?" she flashed, before she could stop herself.

His gaze just briefly met hers. "Is that really how you think of me?"

"You have a big family that loves you, but all you want to do is get away from them. You have no idea how lucky you are, no idea how blessed—"

"And you go through life like the only child you are, Ivy. I never got anything handed to me. I never had one parent's sole attention. Never had new clothes, or a new horse. I grew up fighting for what I wanted, fighting for what I got. So don't lecture me when you're the one that runs away when things don't work out. You're the one that quits too early, not me."

# CHAPTER EIGHT

I VY LAY AWAKE in bed, furious.

And she woke up Sunday morning out of sorts, and when she tried to figure out why she felt so blue, she remembered her fight with Sam last night and it just made her angry all over again.

This wasn't working, being here, being near Sam, trying to act like they were friends when they weren't friends. There was still so much between them… emotion, tension, frustration. There was so much unsettled, so much that confused her.

After a quick breakfast, she went in search of Sam, finding him in the Wyatt's family room, talking to his mom. When she saw she was interrupting, she tried to tiptoe out, but Sam got up and followed her into the kitchen.

"I've been waiting for you to get up," he said, checking the coffeepot and refilling his cup.

Instantly she was on guard. "Everything okay?"

"There was a family meeting last night while I was gone and apparently no one is comfortable with you working at the Wolf Den."

"You want me to leave?"

"No. Why would you say that?"

"Because if everyone is uncomfortable, then I shouldn't be here."

"We're not uncomfortable with you, Ivy. We're uncomfortable with you working there."

"You know I can't just quit."

"Why?"

"Because I made a commitment—"

"Not a good enough reason," he interrupted. "You're not safe there. George doesn't even have a bouncer most of the time. If trouble walks in, you're in trouble."

Ivy paced the length of the kitchen floor. "Trouble hasn't happened yet."

"Your mom wouldn't like it."

She made another face. "You mean, you don't like it."

"No, I don't like it, but your mom wouldn't, either. How often does George come in anymore?"

"Not… often."

"Do you know what he does all day?"

"No, and I don't ask. I'm paid to show up, and so I do."

"Well, I know what he does. He sits at home and drinks and smokes weed—"

"That's his right."

"While you slave away at his bar, taking responsibility for managing things so he doesn't have to."

"It's my job."

"I had no idea you liked it that much."

She glared at him. "*I don't.*"

"Then quit. Let George come in and work. It's his damn bar. If it's that important for the Wolf Den to be open on Christmas Eve and Christmas Day, he can staff it himself."

"But I already agreed to work."

"Come on, Ivy. This isn't about honoring a commitment. It's about punishing yourself."

"Why would I do that?"

"Because Wes did a number on your head, and he's still up there, torturing you. But it's time you put a stop to it. Time to kick him out of your head. Time to take control of your life again."

"I am. I have. I've been saving money, and have a plan. I'm going to be getting my own place soon and I'll be able to start training again. It's going to take some time, but I'm okay with that."

"But I'm not. And Billy and Tommy care about you, a lot. They're concerned, and they've talked to me, and they've decided to cover your shifts for a couple nights, giving George time to hire someone to replace you. Billy will work tomorrow night. Tommy will cover for you Tuesday night, and by then George should be able to hire a replacement. You're not leaving him in the lurch. You're giving him three days' notice."

"Tuesday is your mom's birthday."

"Tommy said he'd rather work, than have you at the

bar."

"Really? I seriously doubt they feel that strongly."

"They do."

"And I doubt they want to work at the Wolf Den."

"They're looking forward to it. They think it's going to be fun."

"Let's go find your brothers. Let me talk to them. Let's see how excited they are about this."

"You don't believe me?"

"I—" She opened her mouth, closed it, then tried again. "I believe you're trying to protect me, but I object to your family being dragged into this."

Sam shook his head. "This is coming from them. Not me."

"I'm going to ask them myself."

"Do that."

"I will." She glared at him as she tugged on her jacket. "And don't come with me. You'll try to influence them."

"I'm going to come with you, but I won't say a word. I won't even look at them. You'll see, too, that I'm not making this up. No one wants you at the Wolf Den. Not Mom, not Grandad, not Joe—"

"Let's just stay focused on the prospective bartenders, shall we?" she said, cutting him off and swinging open the kitchen door to step outside and march to the stables.

SAM DID EXACTLY as he'd promised. He hung back as Ivy entered the ring where Billy and Tommy were practicing on a calf roping dummy, and kept his mouth shut as she charged straight up to them.

"There is no need for you to take on my shifts at the bar," she said, standing between the younger brothers. "I'm perfectly capable working there. I've been working there for almost two months—"

"It's not the right place for a girl like you," Tommy said.

"It's rough," Billy added. "We're not comfortable with you there."

"Sam shouldn't have dragged you into this," she answered.

"He didn't," Tommy answered. "We went to him. We told him we didn't like it. You're practically our sister, and our sister shouldn't be there."

"That's right," Billy echoed. "Bad things happen at the Wolf Den, and maybe they haven't happened yet on your shift, but it's just a matter of time."

Ivy looked from one to the other. "I can handle myself."

"Not saying you can't," Billy said. "But we care about you too much to feel good about you being down there. We're not the only ones. Mom doesn't like it. She worries. And Grandad… you know he doesn't sleep until you're home. And he wouldn't want us telling you, but he thinks of you as a granddaughter—"

"We like feeling responsible for you," Tommy said quietly. "And we like taking care of you. You're important to us. You always have been."

SAM WATCHED AS Ivy turned around and walked quickly out, head down, hands shoved deep into her coat pockets. He let her go, thinking this wasn't the time to chase her down. She needed space and time to process her emotions. Maybe she'd also stop being so stubborn about working at that bar. It was ridiculous, but that was also Ivy. Once she made her mind up about something, it was almost impossible to convince her otherwise.

As the stable door banged shut behind Ivy, he entered the ring where his brothers were practicing roping.

Billy gathered his rope into a loose circle. "Aren't you going to go talk to her?" Billy asked.

"I will. Just giving her a minute," Sam answered.

"You think that's wise? She's pretty upset," Tommy said.

"Your fault, you know," Billy added, throwing his rope, only to quickly pull it back. "You shouldn't have let her go in the first place, Sam."

"It's what she wanted," Sam said gruffly.

Billy rolled his eyes. "I may be allergic to relationships, but even I knew what Ivy wanted. You were just too bull-headed to give it to her."

"I took care of her."

"You talked to your horses more than you talked to her."

Billy made a lasso with his rope, and then snapped it flat. "She wouldn't have left you if you'd given her more attention. We all know it."

"You have no idea how much I loved her."

"True," Tommy said, throwing his rope, circling the dummy. "And maybe she didn't, either."

Sam shook his head and walked out of the arena. He wasn't sure where he'd find her but there weren't that many places she could go. He checked the tack room, she wasn't there, and then he glanced into Scotch's stall, and there she was, brushing Scotch, wiping away tears.

The tears made his head explode. "Why are you crying?"

She looked up, glared at him. "Because I feel like it."

"Everyone is trying to help you, Ivy. We're all trying to show you how much we care."

"Great. Thank you. I appreciate it."

"You don't sound grateful."

She marched toward the door. "I forgot how bossy you are. You're almost as bad as Wes."

"I'm nothing like Wes," he ground out.

"He liked to tell me what to do."

"No one will make you quit the Wolf Den if you love it that much, but we're trying to help you find a way out if that's what you truly want."

"Once I get a new job, I'll give George notice."

"And until then? You're just going to work Christmas Eve and Christmas Day as if there's nothing special about this time of year?"

"Not for me, there isn't. Not when Mom died just a month before Christmas. I don't enjoy it anymore. I don't want to celebrate it, Sam. It makes me sad, okay? Everything about the holiday makes me a little sad. And maybe that doesn't make sense to you, but you've never lost your entire family. Mom was my entire family."

"Maybe I didn't lose my entire family, but I did lose my dad. He died when I was five. And death is awful. Death leaves a huge hole in one's heart. It changes you forever."

"Yes, it does." She wiped another tear away. "So why did you—you, of all people—just send me flowers? You knew how close Mom and I were. You knew she was my best friend. Why didn't you call? Why didn't you come see me? Sam, my dentist sent me flowers. Surely you cared about me more than my dentist?"

"I was trying to respect your grief."

"Seriously?"

Maybe now was the time to tell her everything. She should know the truth. He'd promised Shelby he'd wait two years, or when he thought it was appropriate. Was now appropriate? "Yes, seriously," he answered. "I'm not as insensitive as you think I am."

"That's debatable."

"You want to fight with me?" he drawled. "Let's fight."

"Yes." She swung the door open and stepped out of Scotch's stall. "Let's fight. Let's say all those things we never said before. Let's get it all out in the open so we know why we're not together. I definitely think it's time to clear the air."

He followed her out of the stable. Clouds were gathering in the sky, blocking the sun. "I'm listening, babe. Tell me. I'm all ears."

"You said you loved me. You said you wanted what's best for me."

"Yes. All true."

"Then why let me go?"

"It's what you wanted," he said.

"No."

"*Yes*. You said you couldn't be yourself with me. You said I dominated everything and the only way you could be you, was to get away from me."

"That's not what I said."

"Pretty much."

Tears filled her eyes. "I thought you'd want to discuss it with me. I thought you'd want to resolve the problem with me... not just walk away."

"*I* didn't walk. You did."

"You didn't fight for me."

"And, babe, you didn't fight for us." His gaze met hers, hard, steady. "There was an us, you know, and maybe we weren't perfect, but I'd thought it was good. Really good, actually."

The tears trembled on her lashes. Her mouth quivered.

"Every rodeo was what was best for you. You rarely asked what was best for me."

"I always picked the big money events, and the events that were close to each other. I strategized to make sure we could hit as many events in one weekend as possible. And that wasn't just for me. That was for you, too."

"And yet you'd just announce where we were heading. You never asked me what I wanted."

"Then speak up. Tell me you don't want to go to that event. Tell me which ones you'd rather attend. It's that easy. I can't read minds, Ivy, and as much as I loved you, I couldn't read yours."

IVY HAD TO step back, as Sam's words, *I loved you*, made her chest seize with pain.

It didn't seem fair that the love had been there, but it just hadn't been enough. "I loved you, too," she said quietly, looking out over the frozen pasture. "But we still didn't work out."

"Maybe we took it—and each other—for granted."

She glanced at him over her shoulder.

His broad shoulders shifted. "Just saying you love your horses doesn't mean they'll survive. You've got to feed and water them, exercise them, get them medical care—"

"You don't think I gave our relationship love and care?"

"I think we both gave up too easily. I think we both

failed." Again his gaze found hers, and held. "You're right. I should have come after you, and insisted we have one last proper conversation. I blame myself for that. If I'd done that, then maybe our story would be different now."

She wanted to get up and pace. It took every bit of control she had to stay where she was, and finish this conversation they'd started. "I should have had that conversation, too. I should have told you what I needed. I just thought you… didn't care."

"Didn't care? Ivy, I wanted to marry you."

Her head jerked up, her gaze locking with his.

"I was going to propose to you," he ground out. "I had a ring, but you said you couldn't be yourself with me, that you wanted to be free. I loved you enough to let you go and be free."

Ivy just stared at him, shocked, heartsick. Tears fell, hot, hard. She didn't even try to wipe them away. Instead she just turned around and walked down the road to Joe and Sophie's house with his words, *set you free*, ringing far too loudly in her head.

SOPHIE KNOCKED ONCE on Ivy's door, before opening it slightly to peek inside. "Hey, am I interrupting anything?"

"No." Ivy looked up and forced a crooked smile. "Come in."

Sophie picked her way around the hat boxes and duffel

bag. "What are you doing?" she asked, even as she sat down on the bed, next to Ivy's open suitcase. "Organizing? Or packing?"

"Packing." Ivy wiped her damp face dry. "Or trying, too. Finding it hard to focus, though."

"You don't have to go." Sophie reached into the suitcase and straightened a pile of T-shirts. "You can take some time and think about where you want to go, and what you want to do."

"I had a terrible fight with Sam."

"I heard."

Ivy gave her a stricken look. "It's best if I leave, don't you think?"

"No." Sophie shook her head. "Running away doesn't solve problems. It just prolongs them."

"I have loved Sam from the moment I met him but we can't seem to communicate. We can't make it work and it breaks my heart still."

"I've never seen Sam look at anyone the way he looks at you."

Ivy sank down on the edge of the bed. "I needed him more than he needed me."

"We all have different ways of showing love."

"He just keeps it all inside."

"And you let it all fly." Sophie leaned across the open suitcase and gave Ivy a swift, warm hug. "Don't go. At least not today. Summer and I are going to the Graff for a proper holiday tea. Come with us, please. I've made the reservation for the three of us. You, Summer, and me."

HOLIDAY TEA AT the Graff was a decadent experience and a first for Ivy. She and her mom had never done anything like an afternoon tea before, much less a holiday tea, and after her emotional morning with Sam, she hadn't imagined she'd enjoy tea, but she was wrong. Sitting in a cordoned off section of the hotel's handsome lobby with the tallest Christmas tree she'd ever seen, she felt like special. Spoiled.

Ivy loved the little sandwiches and scones with clotted cream and jam, paired with endless cups of fragrant spice tea while Dickens carolers made their way around the room singing lovely carols put her in a festive mood. She hadn't felt the magic of the Christmas season until now.

"It just feels good to sit," Summer Wyatt said with a contented sigh.

"It does," Sophie agreed, popping a lemon meringue tartlet into her mouth.

"Thank you for including me," Ivy said. "This has been such a treat."

"A much-needed treat for you, I think," Summer answered. "You've been working very hard." Summer cocked her head. "Fighting hard, too, it seems."

Ivy fidgeted. "I'm sorry everyone had to hear that. We should have gone somewhere more private."

"So what's the issue?" Summer asked bluntly. "What's keeping you two from sorting things out?"

"We're just so different. We can't seem to communicate. Every time we try to talk we just end up fighting."

Sophie lifted the teapot from the table and refilled Summer's cup. "Maybe you're talking about the wrong things," she said.

Ivy was baffled. "How can we move forward if we can't clear up the past?"

"You're different people today than you were two years ago," Summer said. "Maybe you just need to forgive and forget."

"Yes, maybe at this point it's time to move on." Sophie studied the tier of little cakes. "Forgive the change of subject, but will anyone mind if I have this last madeleine?"

"I'm done," Summer said, pushing her plate back. "Just tea for me."

"And I don't want it," Ivy said, frowning, thinking of what Sam's mother had said a moment ago. "Maybe I could forgive and forget if I just understood why Sam found it so easy to let me go. If you love someone—"

"You don't break up and walk away to test someone," Summer said, raising an eyebrow. "Why would you test love?"

Ivy blushed. "To make sure it's true?"

Summer regarded Ivy for a long moment, expression thoughtful. "Have you ever considered that the reason your relationship failed, was that you were too insecure?"

The tea, which had been so lovely, turned sour. Ivy put a hand to her lower ribs, stomach churning, matching the pounding in the base of her skull. All of the holiday magic was gone, leaving Ivy feeling naked and ashamed.

"Maybe it wasn't that," Sophie said calmly, filling the strained silence. "Maybe Ivy was confused, and hoped that by breaking up with Sam, she'd get some clarity. Breakups are good for that."

"I certainly didn't mean to lose him," Ivy admitted. "I knew almost right away I'd made a terrible mistake."

"So why didn't you reach out to him?" Summer asked. "Why not tell him you'd made a mistake... offer an olive branch?"

Beneath the table Ivy knotted her hands in her lap. "I should have. I'm not sure why I didn't. I guess I was hurt, and proud."

Summer studied Ivy a long moment, her light blue gaze penetrating. "Maybe this is far-fetched, but it strikes me, Ivy Wyckoff, that you're not as angry with him, as you are with yourself. You have both suffered these past few years because neither of you was willing to face the other and have an honest conversation. I'm not saying the conversation would have changed everything, but at least you wouldn't still be struggling with something that happened two years ago."

Ivy's head throbbed.

The drive back to the ranch felt endless. She closed her

eyes, and rested her forehead against the cold glass, letting Sophie and Sam's mom talk about what they would be doing for Christmas dinner.

Back at the ranch, Ivy slipped away, walking down the driveway to Joe and Sophie's place. Upstairs in her room, she took off her red dress, and then her bra, before pulling a big flannel shirt on. Ivy turned out the light and climbed into bed.

Her head hurt. Her heart hurt. Because Summer was right. Ivy should have had a real conversation with Sam instead of hurling insults. She should still have a real conversation. Being angry was about pride and ego, not about love. And she still loved Sam. She would always love Sam. Even though the two of them couldn't figure out how to communicate.

SAM STOOD ON the front porch staring down the driveway toward Joe and Sophie's house. Ivy hadn't shown up for dinner, and the light was still off in her upstairs bedroom.

He'd wanted to go check on her but his brothers thought maybe Sam just needed to give Ivy space.

Sam sought Sophie's opinion, asking her if it was a bad idea to go check on Sophie.

"She's probably feeling pretty banged up," Sophie answered. "It wasn't quite the festive tea I'd hoped we'd have."

"What happened?" Sam asked.

"You know how your mom gets sometimes. A little intense, a little focused—"

"And a little too direct," Sam concluded, rubbing a hand over his face. "What did she say to her?"

"Nothing that wasn't true. I have to commend Ivy. She handled it all very well." Sophie patted his shoulder. "I wouldn't drag Ivy to dinner tonight. She probably would be happier being alone instead of having to join everyone here."

"What about dinner?"

"I've left some things for her in the kitchen there. She'll be fine."

But dinner was over now and Sam couldn't relax, couldn't stop worrying about Ivy. He'd promised Shelby two years ago he'd take care of Ivy, and he hadn't. He'd done just the opposite, and it wasn't because he didn't care, but he'd cared too much. He'd hated seeing Ivy with someone else. He hated the jealousy, hated the envy. Ivy wasn't supposed to be with Wes. Ivy was supposed to be with him.

Was that why he'd kept his secret so long? Was that why he'd not told Ivy the things he'd wanted to tell her for the last year?

He was going to have to tell her, and the longer he waited, the worse the outcome would be.

Sam walked down the steps of the front porch and headed for Joe and Sophie's cabin. He knew what everyone was telling him, but he also knew he couldn't not go to her.

The front door was unlocked and Sam climbed the stairs.

Ivy's door was closed, the light off. He opened it quietly. He could see a shaft of moonlight on the bed, and then she turned and looked toward him.

"Sam?" she said, her voice sounded rough, husky.

"How are you, babe?" he said, stepping in and closing the door gently behind him.

"I had a headache. Sorry to miss dinner."

"You didn't miss anything. Meat loaf night."

She laughed softly. "I'm sure it was great."

"How is your head now?" he asked.

"Still hurts a little, but it's not as bad."

"Want some pain meds? I can go get you some from the house."

"Sophie gave me some earlier."

"Are you hungry?"

"No. Tea was so rich. I'm still full."

"Heard Mom kind of laid into you during the tea."

"She was fine."

But Sam could see her face in the dark and her eyes looked so sad that it tore him up on the inside. "Scoot over," he said.

She did, and he sat down on the edge of the mattress, and eased off one boot and then the other. Sam stretched out next to her on top of the covers, and wrapped an arm around her. "Is my arm too heavy?" he asked.

"No, it feels good." She snuggled into his embrace. "You feel good."

"I hate fighting with you."

"I don't like it, either."

"So about work tomorrow, you're still planning on it?"

"I didn't tell George I wouldn't be."

"So only an act of God will keep you from showing up tomorrow night."

She huffed a soft laugh. "Probably. Are you praying for one?"

"Oh, I'm praying for a lot of things."

"Good man."

He kissed her temple, inhaling the fresh scent of her shampoo and the smell of her skin. She still felt like his, even after two years apart.

They fell asleep like that, and sometime during the night, Sam woke up, covered by a downy comforter. He looked over at Ivy who'd turned and was facing him, her lips not far from his. He kissed her lightly, and then closed his eyes, and fell back asleep.

# CHAPTER NINE

WHEN IVY WOKE up, Sam was gone, but she knew he'd spent the night with her. His spot was still warm and there was an extra comforter on the bed.

She threw back the covers and went to the window and looked out at a winter wonderland. Snow covered everything, huge white powdery drifts. There was just white in every direction, as far as the eye could see. The fences disappeared, the road and driveway was gone. The roof of the Wyatt cabin showed just how much snow had fallen— the snow had piled up at least two feet—and the snow was still coming down, thick heavy flakes of white.

It seemed Sam's prayers worked.

There would be no way to get down the mountain today. There would be no going to work tonight, not even if she wanted to. The act of God was evident everywhere Ivy turned.

She showered and dressed, and had a cup of coffee in Sophie and Joe's kitchen all while watching the snow fall.

It was beautiful.

Impossibly beautiful.

But chores would have to be done, including taking care of Scotch, and then seeing how she could help in the kitchen. As she finished her coffee, Ivy spotted Sophie emerging from the family cabin, making her way through the swirling snow toward her house.

Ivy opened the door for her. "You look like Frosty," she said, kneeling down to help Sophie get her snow boots off.

"I've never seen it come down like this," Sophie said, hanging her coat up and brushing melting flakes from her cheeks. "It's supposed to keep snowing all day, too."

"What's everyone doing at the house?" Ivy asked, following Sophie back to the kitchen.

"It's just Summer there now. The guys have gone out to check on livestock. Sam, Billy and Tommy saddled up, while Joe and Grandad drove out in one of the four-wheel-drive tractors, carrying out extra hay." Sophie filled up the kettle and moved it on a burner. "Sam wanted me to tell you that he's already fed Scotch. So you don't have to worry about that."

"So what can I do to help?" Ivy offered.

"I was thinking of tackling some holiday baking. I've been putting it off all week, but I have tons of butter, eggs, flour and sugar for cookies and fudge. I also bought some big cans of pumpkin if we have time to make pumpkin bread as that's apparently Grandad's favorite."

"My mom had the best pumpkin bread recipe. She'd make loaves of it every year for neighbors and friends."

"Let's use her recipe."

"I don't have it."

"Maybe it's the one on the back of the Libby's can?"

"Maybe."

"Let's get started on the roll-out sugar cookies, because while that dough is chilling, we can bake the pumpkin bread, and when the pumpkin bread is out, we can pop the cookies in the oven."

For the next couple of hours they worked side by side, first making the sugar cookies, and then two loaves of pumpkin bread, and then while the bread was baking Ivy made a batch of fudge and Sophie began rolling out the cookies on a floured board before cutting them with a set of red plastic cookie cutters.

"My mom had a set of cookie cutters just like those," Ivy said, admiring the stars and trees and angels filling the cookie sheets.

"These are Summer's cookie cutters. She gave them to me, said she'd never be able to use them again." Sophie wiped the flour from her hands and looked up at Ivy. "What shapes should I make next?"

"Santa, stocking, and reindeer."

"Here, your turn to roll," Sophie said, handing over the rolling pin. "I'm feeling a little queasy. I need to sit down."

"You okay?"

"Yes. Just too much coffee on an empty stomach."

"Let me make you some eggs. Or French toast. I make

really good French toast."

Sophie shook her head. "I'll just make some plain old toast in a minute. Do the cookies. I'm fine."

They filled four trays with sugar cookies and as soon as the pumpkin bread came out of the oven, the first pair of cookie sheets went in.

"That pumpkin bread smells so good," Sophie said. "All those spices, yum."

"Let's have a slice," Ivy said. "It's always best warm."

"I guess it won't hurt if we just have a little bit," Sophie agreed. "We don't have to tell anyone."

"No, we don't," Ivy agreed before carefully removing one of the loaves from its baking tin. She used a serrated bread knife to gently cut two slices from the end. "Do you want a bit of butter on yours? That's how Mom and I liked ours."

"Why not?"

Ivy served the pumpkin bread on small plates, and sat down at the table with Sophie. She took a nibble, savoring the flavor. Warm, sweet, moist, flavorful. It was good, but it wasn't quite Mom's recipe. It was almost a little too sweet and not quite spiced enough. She could have sworn her mom's had more cinnamon, clove, nutmeg. Maybe even allspice?

"It's good," Sophie said, finishing her slice. "Don't you think?"

"It is good," Ivy answered, "but I don't think this is the recipe my mom used. Hers was almost like a gingerbread I think, or just had that lovely rich spiced flavor."

Sophie crossed the kitchen and retrieved her iPad that was charging next to her cookbooks. "Let's look up some recipes. Maybe we can figure it out."

"It's okay—"

"No, let's do this. We can make a couple other recipes and see if anything tastes more like hers."

"We'll end up with dozens of pumpkin bread at that rate."

"Great. We'll throw them in the freezer and Grandad can have pumpkin bread all winter long."

SAM SMELLED THE pumpkin bread before he ever saw it. But then he entered Joe and Sophie's kitchen and froze. There wasn't just one loaf of pumpkin bread cooling on the stove. There weren't two. There were at least nine. Maybe ten. And they'd all been cut at one end, with a slice missing from each.

Ivy sat at the kitchen table with a half-dozen recipes around her. Flour dusted her cheek. There was a small orange blob of pumpkin clinging to her long braid.

"What's going on?" he asked.

"Trying to recreate my mom's famous pumpkin bread." Ivy collected the printed recipes, stacking them. "Haven't been successful."

"But I'm sure you've made some good bread."

"Not good enough. It's not hers. I want hers." She

looked up at him, eyes dark with pain. "Everyone said it'd get easier with time, but it's not easier, Sam. It's worse. I missed her last year but it's almost unbearable this year. I can still hear her voice in my head. I can see her in the stable. See her at the fence, coaching me. And I turn, thinking maybe I'll see her, maybe she'll be there. But she's not. Of course she's not."

He sat down at the table and used his knuckles to wipe the flour from her cheek. "You have so much of her inside of you. You're smart like her. Strong like her. Kind like her."

"But it's not enough. There's no closure, Sam. She was here, and then she was gone. And I still can't wrap my head around it."

"And your memories aren't enough."

"No. No. I want her. I want that time I never had with her." She wiped her eyes. "She told me she was getting better, told me everything looked good. It was all lies. She wasn't getting better. She was dying."

"She was trying to protect you."

"How? By telling me lies? By letting me think we'd have so much more time?"

Sam pulled her out of her chair and onto his lap. She let him wrap his arms around her as she buried her face against his neck. He could feel the warm tears fall.

"I was her daughter," she choked. "And she cheated me. She cheated me of being there and taking care of her. I wanted to care for her. Instead, she dies all alone. It kills me,

Sam, to think of her dying without me."

"It couldn't have been easy for her, either," he said, his arms tightening around her. "She was so proud of you, so proud of everything you were accomplishing. She didn't want you home with her, grieving over her. Your mom didn't want anyone crying over her. That wasn't her way."

"I wasn't anyone. I was her daughter. Her *only* child."

"That would have made it all the harder for her, knowing she was leaving you behind. She wanted you to live your life, not count the hours left in hers."

Ivy pulled back, her hazel-green eyes shining, her long black lashes wet. "But that's what *I* wanted. That's what *I* needed. More time with her, not less. And I got less."

This was the moment. This was the moment to tell her. If he didn't do it now, she might never forgive him. "Your mom reached out to me. Toward the end."

"She did this, after we'd broken up?"

He nodded.

"Why?" she said, pain making her voice sharp.

"Because I'd stayed in touch with her."

She exhaled hard. "After we'd broken up?"

"Yes."

"I don't understand."

He carefully removed the pumpkin splatter from her braid. "I liked your mom. She was a great lady. A real cowgirl."

Ivy knocked away a fresh tear before it could fall. "She

never told me." Her voice cracked. "Why wouldn't she tell me?"

"It was between us."

"You two had secrets?"

"A few," he admitted. He opened his mouth, and then closed it, expression grim.

"What?" Ivy demanded.

"Nothing."

She put her hands on his chest, pleading. "Sam, tell me."

"I went and saw her a couple times, just to make sure she had everything she needed. I didn't want her going without, not if I could help her."

Ivy scrambled off his lap. "You got to see my mom, but I didn't?"

"Shelby didn't want you seeing her that way. She was very weak then, very frail."

"You're making me hate you."

His mouth quirked. "That's nothing new, babe."

Ivy turned from him to face the stove with the sea of pumpkin breads. "It's not fair she stayed close to you but pushed me away."

"She didn't push you away. She just didn't let you see her so weak. She must have said a dozen times that she didn't want you remembering her that way."

"And yet she was my mom. Not a cowgirl. Not a hero. Not a barrel racing champion. But my *mom*." Ivy looked at Sam over her shoulder and then back at the pumpkin bread.

"I've been trying so hard to recreate her love, to feel her with me, and all I have to show for it are these loaves of pumpkin bread."

"I bet they're really good."

"They're fine, but they're not hers. I want her recipe. I want *her*." Ivy knocked away more tears. "Oh, Sam, I think I'm losing my mind."

"Let's get out of here. Let's go for a ride."

"There's so much snow."

"The horses would love it. You would, too." He rose. "I'm going to go saddle Scotch and Charlie. Dress warmly and meet me outside."

"I don't know, Sam. I'm worn out."

"Which is exactly why you need to ride."

IVY DIDN'T HAVE it in her to argue and so she went upstairs to change, wrapping a thick cashmere scarf around her neck, the ends tucked into her winter coat, with a wool knit cap on her head and leather fur-lined gloves on her hands.

By the time she was dressed, Sam had the horses saddled and they set off down one of the white powder-coated ranch roads, the horses' hooves muffled by the snow. Sam knew the road well, even though it was hidden, and he led them up the mountain.

The snow was powder soft and the horses sank deep, but as there was no ice, neither horse seemed to mind. Periodically, Ivy would lean forward and pat Scotch's neck, gratified to see his ears slightly back. He was happy, definitely enjoying this time away from the stable. Ivy wasn't happy, but at least she was no longer crying, and there was something infinitely comforting about being in the saddle. She was riding before she could run, and she didn't love just one part of it, but all of it. The motion. The familiar creak of leather. The swish of the horse's tail.

She bent down and pressed her face to Scotch's neck, breathing him in. Every horse had its own unique scent. Belle's smell was probably her favorite, but that was because she was there at Belle's birth and fiercely bonded with her. However, Scotch was a close second. He was smart and brave, and he loved to be challenged. She loved that about him.

Sam steered them right, through what must have been an opening in a gate, across a pristine pasture to a cluster of pines heavily frosted in white.

Beneath the pines was a large rounded boulder, and Sam stopped here, swinging off Charley to tie the reins to a tree. "Let's stretch our legs," he said, reaching into a saddlebag for a thermos and a cup.

"You brought refreshments?" she asked, securing Scotch's reins.

"Hot chocolate. Grandad made it."

Just like that Sophie's throat threatened to seal closed. She blinked, eyes burning. "I think I love him," she said.

"You can love him. I won't mind."

She blinked again and watched as Sam poured hot chocolate in a cup and handed it to her.

"I should have brought marshmallows," he said.

"That's okay. I had so many cookies and pumpkin bread I'm kind of sick."

He smiled and poured himself a cup before capping the cocoa. "Do you mind holding mine?"

"No," she answered taking his cup.

Sam removed a big woolen blanket from the leather straps on the saddle and then spread the red checkered blanket on the boulder. "Sit. Relax. Let's enjoy the view."

She handed him his cocoa and took a seat. It was a stunning view, too. So much white everywhere. Mountains and sky, river and snow. "It's like being at the North Pole," she said, wrapping her hands around her cup. "Just need Santa and his reindeer."

Sam sat down next to her and he used his elbow to nudge her. "I think we've found the reindeer," he said quietly, gesturing to a mature bull elk that had joined them in their frozen winter wonderland.

Ivy's breath caught in her throat. The elk was standing alert, head up, ears twitching, his impressive antlers stark against the clear winter sky. Little by little, other elk arrived until a massive herd filled the pasture, cautiously picking their way through the deep snow, grazing on whatever grass they could find.

"Beautiful," Ivy whispered.

Sam nodded.

The elk glanced at the horses but kept their distance. The horses watched them as well for a bit before losing interest.

For the next half hour, Sam and Ivy watched the herd slowly graze their way across the large open field before disappearing from view.

"Wow. That was amazing," Ivy said. "Really wonderful. Thank you for suggesting we do this. I think sometimes I get into my head too much. I need to get outside more, ride more, do the things that make me feel like Ivy."

"I agree."

"And, Sam, you're right about the Wolf Den. I don't enjoy working there. I don't want to spend Christmas there. But I offered to work those days when I thought I'd be alone."

"But you're not alone. You have me."

She reached out and took his hand, sliding her fingers between his. "I don't hate you."

"I know, babe."

Ivy was content to just sit there next to him, holding his hand.

It didn't matter that her butt was numb and her legs were cold. It didn't matter that she couldn't feel her toes. She was with Sam and it was almost Christmas and she felt a strange peace.

"All that unhappiness," she murmured, "all that pain...

and now we're here." She looked down at their hands and then up into his face. "I don't know what we are anymore, but just being with you feels right. I feel like me."

"If I'd known how unhappy you were—"

"This isn't about Wes, or being with Wes. It's about you. How much I missed you. How much I loved you. How much I hurt being away from you. It was awful. I hated it. I hated that we weren't together… and the feelings were so intense that it…" She swallowed hard. "I felt dead inside."

He said nothing and she forced herself to continue. "Sam, there are only two people I have ever loved in my life. My mom. And you. I maybe loved you imperfectly, but you were pretty much my sun and moon. And in hindsight, I can see that I was naïve. I didn't understand that you have to fight for love, as well as protect love. You can't just take it for granted, or expect it to be easy. I was young and stupid—"

"Not stupid," he interrupted, "but maybe naive. I think we both were. I think we took the love for granted, not realizing what we had was special, and not easy to replace."

"It wasn't, was it?" she murmured.

"No. But that's because there has only been one woman for me, and that's you."

"Crazy," she whispered. "It's crazy that I had no idea how strongly you really felt about me."

Silence stretched, a bittersweet silence that made her stomach burn and her heart ache.

Sam exhaled and kicked at the snow with the heel of his

boot. "I realize now that I didn't say the words enough. I realize I kept my emotions close to my chest. I always have, even as a kid, and I suppose I expected you to know how I felt, based on the things I did for you, based on how I thought I took care of you."

"Based on how you took care of me," she repeated huskily.

"Every time I washed your truck, or hitched the trailer, or filled your tank full of gas, I was taking care of you, making sure you were safe, trying to make your life easier. That was all part of how I tried to show my love, but it wasn't what you wanted, or needed."

"I never thought of it that way." Her hands knotted. "I thought those were just basic things. Chores. Like me making you dinner."

"Which made me feel loved."

Ivy turned to face him. "But you didn't say how much you appreciated it, or how good it was—"

"I didn't know you needed that."

"I always wanted to hear the appreciation, though. I needed you to say, thank you, babe, for dinner. It was awesome. Or, Ivy, I love you."

"I did love you."

"But I needed the words. I needed to feel loved and appreciated."

"Whereas I don't need the words. Your company, it was perfect. It was always enough."

The anger was back, along with the old frustration. Perhaps they really were too different. Perhaps Sam's idea of love wasn't hers. "And I desperately need words."

"If I'd known how much you needed those words, I would have tried harder to share my feelings, and my appreciation." He paused "I'm trying now. But it's not easy opening up. You know talking isn't my forte. And because I might not have the chance to say this again later, let me say now, you're amazing, Ivy. You were born amazing. I was lucky to be in your world, while it lasted."

Her eyes stung all over again. It was beyond tragic to her that their relationship hadn't worked because they hadn't felt duly loved, when the love was there. She turned to look at him, her Sam, with his strong brow, firm mouth, high, hard cheekbones. She loved everything about his beautiful face and impossible heart.

"And I might not have the chance to do this again later, so let me do this now." She closed the distance between them, and reached up to clasp his face, her fingers lightly cupping his warm, bristled jaw. She stroked her thumbs over his chin, and then the hollows beneath his cheekbones before gently putting her mouth to his.

He smelled so good, like love, and home.

The feel of his lips on hers made her heart ache. He still felt like hers. He still felt so very right, as if everything good in the world was here, with her.

She kissed him with love, because that was how she felt

about him. She kissed him with all her heart because for the first time in years, her heart felt whole, and she felt sane. She kissed him as if her life depended on it, because God knew what the future would bring, and all she knew was that this moment was a moment she desperately needed, a moment she'd craved. The kiss deepened and his arms wrapped around her, holding her tight, holding her close, and it was probably the most beautiful, heartbreaking kiss of her life.

So much love.

So much pain.

So much gratitude.

Far better to have loved Sam, and lost him, than to have never loved him at all.

It seemed like forever before he lifted his head, and when he did, she could barely focus, her pulse thudding, her senses dazed.

"You know, you're still my Ivy," he said, his deep voice pitched impossibly low. "You'll always be my Ivy."

"And you'll always be my Sam." Her chest squeezed, her heart filled with pain. "So where does that leave us?"

"It leaves us in a good place, I think. We have the foundation for a future, but I guess the question is, do we both want the same thing?"

DID THEY WANT *the same thing?*

That question went around and around in her head as

they rode back to the Wyatt house. The question continued to eat at her as she ate dinner and then lay in bed, staring at the beamed ceiling of her room.

She suddenly wished she wasn't in a different house than Sam because she wanted to see him, wanted to talk to him, wanted to feel him against her, his arms around her waist, his heart beating beneath her ear.

She reached for her phone and sent him a text. *"Is love enough?"*

*"If you can focus on the big picture and not let the little things get in the way,"* he answered a moment later.

She read his words and thought about it, thought about him, thought about the life she'd wanted with him. *"I agree."*

He responded with, *"Why aren't we together then?"*

Her heart gave a painful lurch. Why weren't they? She hesitated before typing, *"Do you think about us?"*

*"All the time."*

Another painful beat of her heart. *"Could we make it work?"* she asked.

*"Do we want the same thing?"*

*"I think so,"* she answered, before adding, *"I hope so."*

*"Me, too."*

She smiled at her phone, and then kissed the screen. *"Good night, Sam."*

*"Good night, babe. I'm here if you need anything."*

IVY CALLED GEORGE Tuesday morning and told him that she wouldn't be able to work anymore, that she was needed elsewhere, and she was sorry. George grumbled a bit but then accepted her news, letting her know she could pick up her paycheck in a week. Hanging up, Ivy felt a wave of relief. She'd miss the girls at the bar but she wouldn't miss the smell, or the hours, or the endless pick-up lines from all the different guys.

There was still too much snow to get down the mountain, although Sam and his brothers had the big tractor out, and had begun plowing the driveway, and once that was cleared, they were going to start on their private road, scraping away snow three yards at a time.

While the guys worked to clear the road, Ivy and Sophie made Summer's birthday cake, and then later they prepared two huge roasts and twice-baked potatoes for Summer's birthday dinner.

Once the roasts went into the oven, Ivy went to the stable to check on Scotch. He seemed restless and she understood, feeling restless, too. Ivy saddled him and walked him into the arena, delighted to see that three barrels had appeared, positioned on the soft dirt, each twenty-four feet apart.

"Feel like practicing?" she asked Scotch, swinging up into the saddle.

The first time they ran the cloverleaf pattern Ivy felt a little stiff, and Scotch was running slow. But overall it was good. Fun.

She walked him to the start point and they did it again. Scotch flew. Ivy grinned as they rounded each barrel.

That time felt even better.

She felt strong. Free.

They practiced for a good half hour, and it was pure joy to be back riding hard. Scotch just got faster each round, too.

And then they were done, and she walked Scotch to cool him down, before taking him back to his stall to brush him down.

Sam found her in the stable. "Do you want to go see your place?" he asked. "Over in Custer? I don't know when you were last there—"

"Not since I cleared the house out and got it rented."

"Two years ago."

She nodded. "It would be. It was just before Christmas when I sold everything."

"Would it make you too sad to visit, or would it give you any closure?"

"What about my tenants? Won't they mind?"

"You're just checking the place out. You're not moving in."

She thought about it and nodded. "When could we go?"

"Thursday. Tomorrow Joe and Grandad want us to finish plowing the road clear."

"But Thursday is Christmas Eve."

"We could leave in the morning and be back before Santa comes, I promise."

She slugged him and laughed. "Don't make fun of me."

"Seriously, we don't make a big fuss on Christmas Eve, not like you and your mom did. Christmas morning is special in our family and we'll be back in plenty of time to celebrate Christmas with my family."

Christmas Eve *had* been special for Ivy and her mom. In the morning, they delivered meals to those in need and then they'd have a small but special dinner, just the two of them, before they'd each open one special gift.

"I'd enjoy spending Christmas Eve with just you," she said. "It'd make it special for me."

"We'll do that then."

"Your mom really won't mind?"

"No." He kissed the tip of her nose. "Grandad won't either. Or Joe and Sophie. Or Billy—"

"Got it. Thank you."

He laughed and pulled her into his arms and kissed her, a real kiss, a kiss that made her feel alive from head to toe. It was the kind of kiss that made her feel beautiful and loved. Known. And when the kiss ended, she looked up into Sam's eyes, and smiled. He smiled back. It was perfect. No words were needed.

# CHAPTER TEN

THEY LEFT EARLY Thursday morning, so early that most of the family was still asleep, and the sky was still dark. Ivy had filled thermoses with coffee and brought slices of pumpkin bread wrapped in foil for the road. The sun came up as Sam drove, the golden light glorious, rising above the mountains, turning the snowy valley into a glittering landscape.

Sam reached over at one point and took her hand and for the next half hour they just drove, hand in hand.

Sam broke the silence by asking, "Have you heard at all from your dad?"

"You mean since Mom died?"

Sam shot her a concerned look. "It's been that long?"

Ivy shrugged. "I don't think he knows what to do with me."

"But when Shelby died, surely he made an effort then?"

"He couldn't make the funeral, but he did come by the next week."

"How did that go?"

"It probably would have gone better if he'd come on his

own. Instead he brought the whole family. You know, he has a Mercedes SUV. He's all Jackson flash."

"He's a real estate agent, right?"

Ivy nodded. "I guess he's really successful."

"What's his wife like?"

"Nothing like Mom, but nice enough. We couldn't figure out what to say to each other and so I watched Andrea go through the house and pick at all the sympathy floral arrangements, pulling the dead flowers out, while the kids ran around, shooting Nerf bullets at everything."

"How many kids do they have?"

"Five." Ivy laughed. "And they're wild. Serves him right."

Sam shot her an assessing glance. "Does it bother you that he and Andrea have such a big family?"

"No. That's their family. Mom was my family."

"But your dad left you guys."

Ivy chewed her inner lip. "Yeah."

"You never talk about that. If you were eight, you were old enough to know what happened."

"I knew he'd left because he and Mom fought a lot, but I didn't realize when he left her, he also left me. That took me years to figure out."

IVY'S WORDS CLICKED something into place, and Sam finally understood something he'd never understood before.

Maybe the reason she hadn't spoken up all those years ago was that she was afraid she'd lose him. Maybe she hadn't said what needed to be said because she was afraid he'd leave. And maybe she'd left, hoping, praying he'd come for her, proving that once and for all she was valuable. Not someone you'd throw away. Sam drew a breath, aware of a sharp pain in his chest.

He'd thought he understood her. He'd thought he understood everything, but he hadn't seen the big picture. He'd gotten caught up on the little things. He'd focused on the problems not the love.

"How did your mom handle the divorce?" Sam asked.

Ivy combed her ponytail over her shoulder, expression pensive. "Fine. She was happier without him."

"But you weren't."

She sighed, shrugged. "He was Dad."

That just about summed it all up, didn't it? Dads were so important. They couldn't be replaced. Sam glanced at her. "So after the divorce, your father moved to Jackson, made a ton of money in real estate, while you and your mom struggled in Custer?"

"Not exactly. Dad always had money. Mom just didn't want any of it when they divorced. She told him she didn't need anything from him, as long as she had me."

"So he gave you up."

Ivy said nothing.

Sam's chest burned, emotions hot. "You know, Ivy, it's

okay for us to disagree. We can fight, and be fine. I might not like everything you say, but I'm not going to walk out the door. I'm not going to just walk away from you."

"People don't like fighting," she said quietly.

"No, but conflict is part of life. Growing up, my brothers and I fought all the time. We still sometimes get into it. You know I love Grandad, but he and I have had some serious arguments, a couple really serious ones a few years back, but we worked through them. Mom and I had a pretty bad fight the other night, when she wanted you to move over to Joe and Sophie's, but did it change how I feel about her? No. She's still my mom, and I love and respect her."

"Why was she so upset about us kissing? It was pretty tame, you know."

Sam didn't answer right away. "She was pregnant with Joe when she and Dad married. From what I gather, Dad wasn't sure he wanted to get married. He was seeing someone else when Mom traveled from California to Montana, showing up on the doorstep six months pregnant."

"No way."

"Yes, way. Grandad was livid. He had some strong words for Dad, telling him that no Wyatt ever walked away from his child. So Dad manned up, and did the right thing. Fortunately, Dad and Mom worked things out and had a good marriage—" He flashed a grin at Ivy. "Or at least a lot of sex, because they ended up with four boys before he died far too young."

THEY STOPPED FOR gas outside Billings and then forty-five minutes later they were taking the exit for Ivy's childhood home.

Ivy had been okay until they reached the familiar turnoff and then suddenly she felt nervous, her skin prickling hot, then cold as Sam drove down the frontage road.

She sat on the edge of her seat and tried to take it all in. Even covered in snow it was exactly as she remembered. The barbwire fences. The neighbors with their big silos and white barn. And then Sam was turning down the private road to her mom's, and Ivy clenched her hands waiting for the house and stable to come into view.

And then, there it was.

Her house. The place she'd grown up.

"It looks good," she said, her gaze sweeping the property, taking it all in. "But there are no horses. I don't see any livestock at all."

"Maybe they don't have any."

"Then why live here?"

Sam pulled up in front of the house and parked. "Want to get out and walk around?"

"I don't want to cause trouble."

"You won't."

"I should have warned them that I was coming."

"You did." Sam took the key from the engine. "Ivy, I'm your tenant."

"You live here?"

"No. But I've been renting it from you all this time."

"Why?"

"I didn't want you to sell it until you'd had enough time to decide what you were going to do. This was your home after all."

Ivy struggled to take it all in. "You've been paying Wes?"

"Not since September when you wrote and said to not pay anymore. I've been putting the rent aside for you." He opened his door. "Let's get out and walk around."

Ivy walked to the stables with the arena and huge outdoor ring. Everything was immaculate but empty. She turned and looked at Sam, incredulous. "I could be living here now."

"You could, yes. It's an excellent training facility, and has virtually everything you're looking for in Paradise Valley. The only difference is, you already own this."

She looked back at the ring piled with fresh snow. Except here she'd be alone. She wanted to be independent, but she had no one here. She had nothing here but a house and stable and barn. "I'd be lonely here," she said. "And I'm not lonely in Marietta. I've begun to make friends." She glanced back at Sam. "But I do hate that I've wasted your money. You've been saving this for me and as it turns out, I don't want it."

"You didn't waste anything. You learned something important. Now you can sell this place and get something where you'll be happy."

Her heart fell a little, no, make that a lot. She didn't want to be apart from Sam. She'd be happiest with him. "Remember how you said I could go to Cody with you?"

"Yes."

"Did you mean it?"

"Ivy, you don't want to live there."

"I might, if you're there." That didn't quite come out the way she'd intended. "What I'm trying to say is that I want to be where you are. If that offer is on the table. If not, I'll find a place in Paradise Valley to start my horse ranch and I'll have a good life doing what I love to do."

"Of course I want you with me, Ivy. That's a given."

She liked the sound of we, but didn't want to ask too many questions, not yet. Better to just leave the possibility there between them, bright, shiny, hopeful.

"Want to go inside?" he asked, reaching into his pocket and extracting a single key.

"Yes."

The inside of the house looked just like she remembered, but only better. The wood paneled walls were scrubbed clean, and the hardwood floor had a rich polish on it. The house had no furniture, but there were a few pictures on the wall, framed photos of her favorite horses, and even better, photos of Ivy's mom.

Ivy stopped and breathed in, smelling the lovely scent of fresh pine. Her pulse quickened, and she looked at Sam and then headed down the hall, passing the dark kitchen. As she walked, Sam flipped a switch, and a Christmas tree in the corner lit up.

The tree was in the same corner she and her mom had always put it in, although this wasn't a tabletop tree, but a tree close to seven feet tall and covered with hundreds of white lights. There were so many lights that it made her chest so tender it hurt to breathe.

"Did you do this?" she asked.

"Yesterday."

"And I thought it just took forever to clear the road."

"Billy and Tommy came with me. They helped me get the tree up."

She moved to the tree and, reaching out, touched the first ornament that caught her eye. A bronze horse. She looked at another ornament, and it was a horse. Every ornament was either a red glass ball or a horse. She recognized one of the horses, but not all. "Where did you find all of these?"

"We went to every toy, antique and feed store between Livingston and Billings, and bought every horse we could find."

"Your poor brothers."

"They loved it. To them it was one big adventure."

"Or you bribed them."

He grinned. "Or I bribed them." His smile faded and his gaze narrowed, and he stood there suddenly serious. "There is one gift under the tree for you, too."

"But I don't have anything for you."

"This isn't from me. It's a gift from your mom. She asked me to wait and give it to you at Christmas. I tried last year, I mailed it to you at Wes's, but it came back to me."

"He rejected it?"

"Seems so."

She looked at the tree, searching for the mysterious present. "And you kept it for me."

"I did."

"Do you know what it is?"

"I have an idea, but I've never opened it, so I could be wrong."

Sam reached around the back of the tree and pulled out a box and handed it to her. The box had her name on it, and Wes's address, as well as a big inked RETURN TO SENDER across the front.

"It's the right address," she said. "I don't know why it was rejected."

"I'm just glad it did come back. I'm glad it didn't end up in the garbage somewhere." Sam pulled out a pocketknife and slit the tape on the box, before pulling out a bright red foil package with an envelope taped to the front.

Ivy took the present and looked down at the envelope. Her name was written on the envelope in her mother's cursive, although the handwriting was spidery and thin. She pressed the envelope to her chest, pressing her mother's handwriting to her heart. "I'm scared to open it."

"Don't be scared."

"But she did this for me before she died?"

He nodded.

Ivy looked at him a long moment before opening the envelope and drawing out the Christmas card featuring a chestnut horse in the snow, with a wreath around its neck.

The horse looked just like Belle and Ivy felt a lump in her throat.

*Ivy,*

*I hope you have forgiven me for keeping the severity of my illness from you. It didn't seem right to have you grieve while I was still alive. Maybe it's selfish, but I didn't want to spend the little time I had left, discussing death. Instead I wanted to use every minute to focus on what gives me pleasure—you, your career, and your beautiful gift with horses.*

*My hope is that you will find your way back to love. If you've taught me anything, it's that love shouldn't make one weak. Love should make one strong.*

*Don't be afraid to seize life and make the most of it. You deserve every joy. I will be forever cheering you on.*

*Your biggest fan,*
*Mom*

Ivy closed the card and just held it, emotion washing through her in waves. "That was intense," she whispered, looking up at Sam.

He said nothing and she opened the gift, peeling away the red foil paper to reveal a bubble wrapped phone and charger. She unwrapped the phone, not recognizing it. Her mom always had one of those cheap throwaway phones, hating to waste money on expensive technology, never mind big contracts. "What's the phone for?" she asked Sam.

"Let's plug it in," he said, leaning across her to take the charger and plug it in the wall next to all the Christmas lights.

It took a minute for the phone to charge sufficiently to turn on. There was no lock on the phone, and very few apps. Basically the only thing on the phone seemed to be a folder with the name *Ivy*.

Ivy opened the folder and dozens of video icons appeared. She scrolled through them noting they were all dated, and she went to the oldest video, and tapped on the very first one, a video dated five months before her mother's death.

The video began. Her mom came to life, thin, almost gaunt, her thick dark hair shot with silver, her expression somewhat self-mocking, as she spoke awkwardly, self-consciously into her phone.

*Hi, Ivy, it's Mom. I know this is weird. It's a little weird for me, too, but there is so much I wanted to tell you, but I've been afraid that if I did, you'd want to come home, and I didn't want that. You don't need to be here, you need to be out living your life. This is your time, and this is your year. And I refuse to let me being sick, interfere with your best year, and what a year it is. So proud of you, Ivy. You and Belle are having an incredible year. Give your girl a big kiss from me.*

And then another video, a few weeks after that. *Ivy, I watched you ride tonight on TV and I couldn't have been prouder. Just keep that hat brim level and you'll be bringing home a lot more trophies.*

Ivy skipped forward to one of the last videos. Her mom was beyond thin. She looked gray, skeletal, and yet her hazel eyes were clear and her voice steady.

*Ivy, I knew this was your year. I could feel it in my bones. I would love to see you ride in Las Vegas this year, but at least I have seen you ride almost every weekend.*

*I am dying, Ivy. There is nothing to be done now. There is nothing anyone can do. I have tried everything, and I have fought hard, but the time to fight is over.*

*I've been told I have a few weeks, but it could also be days, and so I'm cleaning out the house, trying to prepare things so it will be easier for you once I'm gone.*

*So no tears, no grieving, no fuss. You know how I hate fuss. Be strong for me. I love you so much, more than you'll ever know.*

*Your forever fan,*
*Mom*

Ivy put down the phone, and walked out of the living room, grabbing her coat on the way. She walked across the yard to the old barn. The barn was quiet and cool and, even empty, still smelled of hay and feed. She slipped into the stall that used to be Belle's and sat on the ground, knees pulled up to her chest and rested her head on her knees and cried.

And cried.

She cried until she couldn't cry anymore.

Her eyes felt swollen and her nose was running and she took an old crumpled tissue from her coat pocket to wipe her nose and try to dry her face.

Time passed—she had no idea how much time—until little by little she realized she wasn't alone. Even though it was almost dusk, she could feel Sam there, outside the stall. She had no idea how long he'd been there, but suspected it had been awhile. "Go away," she said hoarsely.

"No."

"I don't want you here."

"Yes, you do."

"Not right now." She hiccupped, and drew a rough, raw breath. "I am so mad at you. *So* mad."

"I know."

"You had this all this time. You had this card and these videos… You had everything I needed."

"I know."

"Did you know what was in this envelope?"

The stall door creaked as he leaned on it. "I didn't know

about all the videos. I knew about one, because she asked me to hold the phone and record the last one."

For a long time Ivy couldn't speak, filled with far too many intense emotions, overwhelmed by her racing heart and the pain splintering inside of her. "How did she die? Who was with her? Was she alone?"

"No."

"Who was with her at the end?"

Sam didn't even hesitate. "I was."

Ivy exhaled hard, eyes on fire, heart on fire. She didn't know if she loved him or hated him in that moment. "Please tell me. Please tell me what happened… at the end."

"It was all very calm, very quiet. That morning she made her last video for you, and then said she was tired. I took her hand and she closed her eyes. After a couple of hours she was gone."

"You were holding her hand when she died?"

"Once I took it, I never let it go."

Ivy felt raw anguish, but also relief. Thank God. Thank God Sam had been there, sitting with her. "She wasn't in pain?" Ivy whispered.

"She'd been given morphine, but she was fairly lucid that morning. She knew I was there. She wanted to make a last video."

Fresh tears filled Ivy's eyes. All this time she'd feared her mom had suffered. She'd worried her mom had been afraid. But to know that Sam had been there helped immensely. If she couldn't be there, there was no one else she would have wanted with her mom, but Sam.

Strong, honest, loyal Sam Wyatt.

Her Sam Wyatt.

"It couldn't have been easy for you," she said huskily.

"It wasn't hard, because I loved her, and I love you."

Ivy's chest burned. Her throat felt raw. She rested her head on her knees, wiping tears that fell. Today had been a day of surprises and revelations but it also explained some things, giving closure. "I still should have been there."

"I agree." Sam's voice deepened. "If I could do it over again, I'd call you. I'd ask you to come. I wouldn't let your mom's feelings be more important than yours."

"She's hard to say no to."

"You're telling me."

Ivy looked up, rubbed at her cheeks. Her face felt swollen. Her eyes burned. Her nose burned. She felt as if she'd been hit by a truck. "Can I ask you about one more thing?"

"Absolutely."

"You said you love me, not loved. Not past tense. But love."

"Yes."

She studied him in the dim light. "Do you mean that?"

"Yes."

She extended a hand, and he took it, pulling her easily to her feet. Facing him, she searched his blue eyes. "Platonic love or…"

"Or." The corner of his mouth lifted. "Most definitely or."

Ivy blushed. "I'm glad, because my feelings are not at all platonic, either. I'm crazy about you, Sam. I love you so much."

Sam carefully wiped the tears drying on her cheeks. "I know."

"You do?"

"You're not that hard to read."

"Oh."

"I do have a solution, though."

"Yeah?"

"Marry me. Let's stop this madness and get married soon."

"How soon?"

"After Christmas."

Her brow creased. "You're closing your place after Christmas."

"But I'll be back before New Year's."

"We could get married New Year's Eve, or New Year's Day—"

"How do we plan a wedding in a week?"

"Keep it small, just family. Or, we could go to the courthouse, get married by a judge like Joe and Sophie did."

"That's not romantic. Why not at the ranch?"

"As long as it's not in the stable. I know how much you love horses."

Ivy laughed, amused, and beyond happy. "But you are serious, right? You really want to marry me?"

"Yes. Next week. Why wait? You love me. I love you. We're meant to be together."

"We are," she agreed. "I just hate that I let my pride get in the way.

"We both did," he said.

"But we're not the same people we were before," she said quietly.

"No, we're not. We've changed." He pushed back a tendril of her hair from her cheek. "Do you feel rushed into marriage, though? If you're not ready—"

"I'm ready. I just wonder if *you* think I need to be on my own awhile. Maybe prove that I'm able to be independent, that I don't need anyone."

He made a rough raspy sound that sounded an awful lot like muffled laughter. "Is that what you want to do? Prove to me you don't need me? Because I thought that's what you've been doing for the past couple of years."

"Unsuccessfully," she muttered, putting her hand on his chest to push him away but then stroking the hard muscular plane over his heart. He felt so good. He felt like everything she'd ever wanted, and missed. "Wes—"

"Do we really have to talk about him? I hate him. I want to put my fist into his face and keep doing that until—"

"Okay, let's not talk about Wes." She kissed Sam's chin, and then rose up on tiptoe to kiss his lips. "And you're not just saying you love me and want to marry me because you saw me crying my eyes out in Belle's old stall?"

"Was this her stall?"

Ivy nodded.

"I'm sorry. I know you loved her." And then he hugged her. "Incidentally, I'm proposing for purely selfish reasons. I'm crazy about you, and I miss you. I want you back where you belong… in my life, in my truck, in my bed."

"And your heart?" she asked hopefully.

He stroked a tendril of hair back from her brow. "Babe, you never left my heart. You've been there every moment of every day for the past two years. Trust me when I say I've had a heck of a time figuring out how to live without you."

"Then don't."

THEY STOPPED FOR dinner at a diner in Billings, and then continued on to Pray, arriving back on the ranch late. All the lights were still on, but now that they'd reached the Wyatt Ranch, Ivy wasn't ready to go inside. "Can we just talk for a minute?" she asked as he parked next to his brothers' trucks.

"Of course."

"You're still going to close on your Cody ranch."

"Yes."

"So shouldn't we go live in Cody then? It's what you'd wanted—"

"Ivy, no. It wouldn't be good for you, and it wouldn't be

good for your business. I'm pretty isolated. It's land, great land, but there aren't any neighbors, and there wouldn't be little girls to train."

"I'm sure I could find someone."

He smiled. "I'm sure you could, but that's not the point. I want you to be happy."

"Sam, I'll be happy wherever you are."

"But I won't be happy if I take you from here."

"And yet neither of us have a place here."

"So we sell both of our places, and buy a new ranch together, something that we will both like. Something that will meet both of our needs."

Ivy felt a stirring of excitement. "Where would we look for a place?"

"I think we've already been looking at places together, places we liked."

"You mean on Saturday? When we were driving around looking at horse ranches before we went to Ashley's?"

"We saw a couple places we both really liked."

Ivy immediately thought about the gorgeous place up near Clyde Park. "Some of them were very expensive."

"A few were, but when we pool our resources, and sell the other properties, we'll be able to afford a nice place. Maybe even one of those 'dream places.'"

The bubble of excitement grew within her. Options and possibilities sparkled. Ivy liked to think she was pretty grounded, but right now she felt as if she'd drunk a bottle of golden champagne. Everything felt fizzy and light within her. "But those places—regardless of price range—they're all rather close to your family's ranch." She looked at him, trying to keep her expression neutral. "And I know you don't want to live in your family's back pocket. You said you wanted space, and a chance to be your own person. I'm worried that getting a place in Park County or Crawford County might be too close to the Wyatt Ranch."

"I don't have to be hours away from them. Thirty minutes, forty-five, that could be okay. It'd be nice to be able to join everyone for a birthday dinner, or even just a Sunday family dinner, because you're right, I won't have my mom and grandad forever. Who knows what the future will bring? Things happen, accidents and illness happen, and the most important people in my life are you and my family. And I don't want to lose you, and I don't want to lose them, and if Joe and Sophie have a baby, I want to be a good uncle. If you and I have kids, I want my kids to know their relatives."

"Yes." She leaned into him. "I agree with every word you're saying."

He smoothed her hair back from her brow, his thumb stroking her cheek. "Yeah?"

"We're going to have our own place," she said happily.

"Yes."

"And when we're done competing, we'll be able to do the things we love. Cattle, horses, family."

He kissed her. "Best of all, it's going to be you and me."

# CHAPTER ELEVEN

I VY WAS STILL asleep when Sophie knocked on her bedroom door. "Merry Christmas," Sophie said, opening the door. "Wake up, sleepy head."

Ivy groaned, not wanting to wake. She'd been in the middle of the most wonderful dream. She and Sam had married and had found a house and they were raising her horses and competing again, and they were so very happy. "What time is it?" she asked, yawning and stretching.

"Seven thirty and breakfast will be ready soon. Everyone's waiting for you."

"There's no sleeping in around here."

"On a ranch or farm? Come on, you know better."

Ivy dressed and headed over to the main house. Christmas breakfast was just as noisy, boisterous and high-spirited as every other meal at the Wyatt house. Tommy and Billy were in particularly fine form too, teasing, bantering, having a painfully good time at everyone else's expense.

Ivy sat next to Sam, and he held her hand under the table. She didn't have much appetite, still giddy from the night before. Were they really getting married? Would they marry soon?

She was ready, more than ready, to take this next step, anxious to make up for lost time. The last few years had been hard but they'd taught her invaluable lessons, lessons that would help her the rest of her life.

At some point, she'd watch the rest of the videos from her mom, but she'd wait until she was ready for that. The videos were a lovely gift, but they weren't easy, bringing back the pain and loss. Worse was seeing her mom waste away over the final months of her life. Maybe she didn't need to watch them all. She had memories of her mom, good memories she carried within her, and maybe that love was enough.

After breakfast everyone topped off their coffee and headed into the living room for stockings and gifts. There were stockings at the mantel for everyone, including Melvin and Summer. Tommy passed the stockings out then and even found one with Ivy's name on it.

The felt stockings were lumpy things and Ivy smiled as Sam's brothers emptied theirs. It was exactly what you'd expect grown men to get. Socks, boxers, razors, shaving cream, along with some fruit, gum, and candied nuts. Billy immediately peeled his mandarin orange and began to eat it. Tommy wasted no time opening his candied pecans.

Sam gave her a little nudge. "Aren't you going to see what's in yours?"

Ivy smiled. "Yes. I'm just savoring it all. This is really

lovely. I've never had a Christmas like this."

"Come on, Ivy, open your stocking. Let's see what kind of underwear Santa brought you," Tommy said.

Sam immediately gave him a dirty look. Tommy and Billy laughed. Even Joe was smiling.

Blushing, Ivy ignored them. "What did you get in your stocking, Sophie?" Ivy asked, fairly sure that she and Sophie had been given the same things.

"I haven't opened mine yet either," Sophie said. "I'm not sure I'm brave enough."

"You'll be okay," Joe said. "I won't let anything happen to you."

Sophie reached into her stocking and pulled out a knit cap, hand lotion, ChapStick, fruit, and candy nuts. And then she reached back in and, brow furrowed, she pulled out a colorful plastic baby rattle.

The room went quiet.

Joe took the plastic rattle from Sophie. "What is this?"

Ivy slowly smiled. She glanced at Sam and he smiled at her. She smiled back. Sophie was pregnant.

Looking around the room everyone seemed to understand but Joe. He was baffled. "I don't get it," he said.

Sam laughed. "Joe, think about it."

Sophie leaned close to Joe and whispered in his ear. He jumped to his feet. "We're having a baby?"

Sophie nodded. "He or she will be coming late May."

"I can't believe it. You're serious?"

She nodded. "I didn't know what to get you for Christmas, so I thought… why not a baby?"

Everyone laughed, and Joe and Sophie disappeared from the room and everyone talked about the first Wyatt baby in twenty-something years. Ivy was caught up in the excitement as well. Sophie and Joe would be such great parents.

And then Grandad spoke up, making himself heard over the hum of voices. "Ivy hasn't yet opened her stocking. Ivy, it's your turn."

Ivy reached into her stocking and pulled out a scarf and mittens set, a mandarin orange, candied nuts, hand lotion and ChapStick, and then, reaching back in, she felt a little square box. The box felt like velvet. She pulled it out; the box was black and very elegant. She held it in her hands a moment, afraid to open it and be disappointed. What if it wasn't a ring? What if it was a necklace or earrings—which of course would be lovely—but what she wanted, more than anything, was an engagement ring.

Sam took the box from her, and opening it, he knelt in front of her.

Ivy heard Tommy and Billy shout, but she only had eyes for Sam.

"Ivy, will you marry me?" he asked.

It was the most simple of words, straight and to the point, and yet they were absolutely perfect. Ivy leaned forward, clasped Sam's handsome face between her hands. "Yes, oh yes, yes, yes," she cried, before kissing him.

Sam slid the ring on her finger and Ivy began to cry.

"She's not pregnant, too, is she?" Billy said loudly, wanting to be heard.

Summer gave Billy a frosty glare but everyone else burst into laughter. Ivy laughed, too, thinking this was just possibly the best Christmas ever.

IVY COULDN'T STOP looking at the gorgeous diamond ring on her fourth finger. All morning, all afternoon she'd pause to admire it. She was engaged. She was *engaged*, to Sam, *her* Sam.

Her happiness was almost overwhelming. It might have been a hard year or two, but all the ups and downs, all the heartache and trouble, somehow had come together for something wonderful, something magical.

She'd found her way back to Sam. And he loved her. She knew, this time, just how much he loved her, too. There was no question in her mind. No doubt. Just peace and joy.

She'd learned a lot about love as well, understanding that love wasn't necessarily a fragile thing, nor was it a wish or dream. If anything, love was a muscle, and it required action. It required practice. It required patience and understanding, too.

She knew now that it wasn't enough to just love. She had to grow and desire to do better. Love stronger. Love even when she didn't feel love, and love even when things were hard.

After dinner, and two hours of playing Hearts, Ivy headed outside to stretch her legs, wanting some fresh air. She found her coat and gloves on the hall coatrack, and added the new scarf she'd gotten in her stocking, wrapping it loosely around her neck. In her coat pocket was a small apple she'd taken from the fruit basket earlier.

As the Wyatts talked and laughter filled the house, she opened the front door and slipped outside. Ivy walked away from the ranch house, boots crunching snow, hands buried deep in her coat pockets. She walked until she was swallowed by the tall snow-frosted trees and completely alone. Once hidden from the house, she looked up at the dark sky studded with stars and sent a silent greeting to her mom.

Her mom would have enjoyed this Christmas. Her mom had always liked the Wyatts, and she obviously loved Sam. Ivy was certain her mom had played a role in getting her and Sam together. Even now, she could feel her mom's spirit all around her. *"Thanks, Mom,"* she whispered. *"Merry Christmas."*

Ivy headed back toward the house, stopping at the stable on the way. She'd visited Scotch earlier this morning, but the visit had been far too short with all the festivities going on and she wanted to give him the apple as a small Christmas treat.

Inside the stable, she breathed her favorite scent of leather, feed, and hay. She walked toward Scotch's stall but he didn't immediately look at her. Ivy gave him a pat, and then looked past his head to see what had gotten his attention.

In the stall next to his was Belle.

*Belle.*

Ivy's legs went weak. She couldn't move. Her legs could barely hold her.

Belle spotted her. She nickered. Once and again.

Heart racing, Ivy went to her beautiful girl. She stroked Belle's cheek and then her soft velvety nose. Belle nuzzled her, pressing her face against Ivy's shoulder, huffing as if to say hello. Ivy was determined not to cry again today. She cried when she'd gotten the ring. But oh, this was Belle, and she was here in the Wyatt stable, which could only mean one thing. Sam had bought her back. Sam had moved mountains for her, Ivy Wyckoff.

"Merry Christmas, babe," Sam's deep voice came from behind her. "Hope it's a good one."

She turned around and flung herself into his arm. "The best, Sam Wyatt. Absolutely the best." Then he was kissing her, and it was truly the most perfect Christmas ever.

# EPILOGUE

T HEY MARRIED LATE afternoon on the front lawn of the Wyatt Ranch, the frozen grass covered in a glittering layer of fresh snow. The sweeping Gallatin mountains provided a dramatic backdrop while the inky-blue Yellowstone River snaked far below. Sophie and Grandad created an arch for the ceremony, and then Sophie covered the arch with fragrant greenery and pink and red flowers. The romantic arch created an air of rustic elegance, perfect for the intimate celebration.

For a wedding ceremony on the last day of December, Sam wore a cowboy hat, an oatmeal tweed blazer with a darker vest beneath. He'd paired his blazer to go with his best dark denim jeans, and his favorite dress boots. A simple red rose served as his boutonniere.

Ivy and Sophie had driven to Bozeman the day after Christmas and found a vintage wedding gown that only needed a couple of seams taken in to fit Ivy like a glove. The vintage bridal gown was reminiscent of a classic ball gown with a sleek crepe bodice, long narrow sleeves and a bateau neckline that tapered into a full, frothy tulle skirt. In the gown, Ivy felt like a princess, and she, too, wore boots, but she wore her favorite battered brown boots to remind herself to dream big, but also always keep her feet firmly planted on the ground.

Ivy plaited her hair into a long loose fishtail braid with a few loose tendrils to frame her face. Sam's mom had given her a pair of her own Montana sapphire earrings to wear, and Ivy carried her mother's leather-bound prayer book, the book tucked behind her crimson and pink floral bouquet.

Sophie served as Ivy's sole bridesmaid, while Joe stood up with Sam. The only guests were immediate family and the justice of the peace made it a quick ceremony to keep Melvin and Summer from standing too long in the cold. A photographer the Wyatts knew, McKenna Sheenan, took photos, capturing Ivy and Sam's happiness.

After the vows were said, the sun began to set, creating glowing golden light behind the luminous mountain peaks. Joe brought out bottles of chilled champagne while Sophie retrieved a silver tray of champagne flutes. With Summer seated in a rocking chair, snugly wrapped in blankets, toasts were made, and glasses clinked, and Ivy and Sam kissed, and laughed, and kissed yet again. After the drama of the past week, and all the heart-wrenching revelations, Ivy had wondered if she'd feel strange getting married so quickly. She'd wondered if Sam would feel any regret, but every time he kissed her, he murmured, "I love you, Ivy girl." Her heart did that furious double beat and she felt only love and gratitude. They'd found their way back to each other. They'd found their way back to love. If there was any regret, it was that Mom wasn't here physically, but Ivy felt her spirit surrounding them.

"She wanted us to be together, didn't she?" Ivy asked, wrapping an arm around Sam's waist, as they stood at the railing and watched the sun go down together.

"She knew I loved you. She knew I'd always take care of you."

Ivy snuggled closer. "I think she knew how much I loved you."

"Soul mates with a little trouble communicating."

She smiled and glanced up, her eyes meeting his. "You make me laugh."

"Better than making you cry."

She laughed again and then her laugh turned into a sigh as his head dropped and his lips covered hers in a slow, bone-melting kiss. Their kiss was ended by loud whistles and a chant of "Get a room."

Sam lifted his head and made a face at his brothers.

Ivy arched an eyebrow. "They have a point. Where am I sleeping tonight?"

"My room," Sam answered. "And then tomorrow we'll start looking for our own place."

They were called to dinner then, and they went inside to sit down at the dining room table, the table covered with antique lace, and the best china and crystal from Grandma

Wyatt. The napkin rings were bronze horses and the flowers were the same lovely reds and greens and pinks from the arch. They feasted on French onion soup, prime rib, mashed potatoes and gravy, and an assortment of salads and vegetables. For the dessert, it was chocolate mousse and wedding cake.

Ivy teared up as she gazed around the table, thinking this was the best wedding she'd ever been to. How could anything be better? She was with Sam and her new family… the people she loved best.

## THE END

Want more? Check out Billy and Erika's romance in
*Montana Cowboy Daddy*!
Pre-order now!

Join Tule Publishing's newsletter for more great reads and weekly deals!

# THE WYATT BROTHERS OF
# MONTANA SERIES

Book 1: *Montana Cowboy Romance*

Book 2: *Montana Cowboy Christmas*

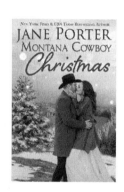

Book 3: *Montana Cowboy Daddy*
Pre-order now!

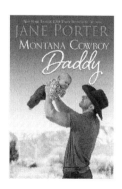

# MORE BY JANE PORTER

## Love on Chance Avenue series

Book 1: *Take Me, Cowboy*
Winner of the RITA® Award for Best Romance Novella

Book 2: *Miracle on Chance Avenue*

Book 3: *Take a Chance on Me*

Book 4: *Not Christmas Without You*

## The Taming of the Sheenans series

The Sheenans are six powerful wealthy brothers from Marietta, Montana. They are big, tough, rugged men, and as different as the Montana landscape.

### Christmas at Copper Mountain
Book 1: Brock Sheenan's story

### Tycoon's Kiss
Book 2: Troy Sheenan's story

### The Kidnapped Christmas Bride
Book 3: Trey Sheenan's story

**Taming of the Bachelor**
Book 4: Dillion Sheenan's story

**A Christmas Miracle for Daisy**
Book 5: Cormac Sheenan's story

**The Lost Sheenan's Bride**
Book 6: Shane Sheenan's story

*Available now at your favorite online retailer!*

# ABOUT THE AUTHOR

New York Times and USA Today bestselling author of over fifty five romances and women's fiction titles, **Jane Porter** has been a finalist for the prestigious RITA award five times and won in 2014 for Best Novella with her story, Take Me, Cowboy, from Tule Publishing. Today, Jane has over 12 million copies in print, including her wildly successful, Flirting With Forty, picked by Redbook as its Red Hot Summer Read, and reprinted six times in seven weeks before being made into a Lifetime movie starring Heather Locklear. A mother of three sons, Jane holds an MA in Writing from the University of San Francisco and makes her home in sunny San Clemente, CA with her surfer husband and two dogs.

Thank you for reading

## Montana Cowboy Christmas

If you enjoyed this book, you can find more from all our great authors at TulePublishing.com, or from your favorite online retailer.

TULE
PUBLISHING

Made in the USA
Coppell, TX
13 April 2022

76545723R00157